"A cou... and a city-bred man.

Dana's voice rose over the sound of the shower. "Met on the highway one fateful night."

Garth shook his head and unbuttoned his shirt. Whatever the tune was supposed to be, Dana was fracturing it. Off went the shirt, then his shoes.

"Oh, country and city, they're worlds apart. But—"

He dropped his pants on the floor. "Country and city—" he sang, imitating her twang "—will git along fine."

Dana watched as he pulled back the curtain. He was gorgeous, his body lean and sinewy. . . and aroused.

"Stop worrying about our differences," he soothed, stepping in and blocking the spray. His eyes moved over her shimmering wet body before he drew her close.

He was hard and hot, and an equally fiery heat flowed through her. Looking up, Dana smiled. "You know," she said in a husky voice, "I'm really beginning to appreciate those differences. . . ."

Maris Soule's first published book
helped launch the Temptation line in
1984. Since then she has become a
seasoned pro, regularly contributing
distinctive stories to Temptation. The
broad range of subjects—from barrel
racing to fine art—that Maris presents
with such authority reflects her own
varied interests and talents. As for her
love of romance, Maris sees that as a
reflection of the fact that she's been
married for almost twenty years and is
"still in love." Two children complete the
happy Soule household
in Michigan.

Books by Maris Soule

HARLEQUIN TEMPTATION

The Best of Everything

MARIS SOULE

Harlequin Books

TORONTO • NEW YORK • LONDON
AMSTERDAM • PARIS • SYDNEY • HAMBURG
STOCKHOLM • ATHENS • TOKYO • MILAN

Published June 1988

ISBN 0-373-25306-0

1

As the amber lights of the tow truck flashed—circles of orange against a sky of fading blue—Dana Allen held her breath and watched the boom and tow-cable pulley rapidly coming close. The way things were going, she wouldn't be the least bit surprised if the truck backed right into her pickup. A crumpled front fender would be just one more hitch in her plans. Being stuck on the side of the freeway certainly hadn't been on her agenda.

The tow truck stopped only inches away, and Dana breathed a sigh of relief, then slid out from behind the steering wheel. The other driver took his time getting out, glanced up and down the highway, then sauntered toward her. "You the one who called?"

"Yeah." She'd had to walk a mile before she found a telephone, but at least she'd found one.

"You said you thought you had a wheel-bearing going out."

"I don't think it's going out; it's gone. Right front wheel," she explained, pointing.

Dana watched him amble around to the right side of her truck and look at the wheel. He was dressed in grease-stained, worn blue coveralls, the name Garth stitched above the top pocket. His brown hair was thick and unruly, as though he'd run his fingers through it often, and a five-o'clock shadow darkened his chin. He looked as if he'd put in a long day, and she knew he hadn't come willingly. It had taken her ten minutes on the telephone to convince him to help her.

Curious, Garth looked over the rusted Ford pickup. Its faded blue paint was covered with dust, the blue and white cap over the bed was dented and a deep scratch extended from the driver's door to the tailgate. It looked in far worse shape than the silver-and-black horse trailer it was pulling. "Does the engine turn over?" he asked across the hood of her truck.

"It's not the engine." She was getting exasperated. "The problem's there, in the wheel . . . a bearing, I'm sure."

There was a movement in the trailer and the sound of hooves on flooring. Garth glanced that way. "You got a horse in there?"

"Yes. I'm racing him tomorrow night." At least that had been her plan up till an hour ago. Now she wasn't sure what she'd be doing in the next twenty-four hours.

"A racehorse, eh? Has he won many races?" Garth strolled back to the driver's side of the truck.

"A few. He's a barrel-racing horse." Windrunner had won more than a few contests, but at the moment Dana didn't feel like discussing the matter. She simply wanted to get to the next rodeo.

Garth opened her truck door and in one fluid motion swung up behind the wheel.

His actions took her by surprise. Even more surprising was the sound of her engine turning over. "What are you doing?" she demanded. She knew the problem wasn't with the motor.

"Checking out your truck." For a second he listened, then released the brake and put the gears into reverse.

"Wait! Don't!" Dana took two running steps, waving her arms, then stopped. He wasn't paying any attention to her. Chasing after him wasn't going to help; in fact it might distract him. Chewing on her lower lip, fingers crossed, she watched nervously. He'd better know what he was doing. The cars passing them were going at least sixty miles an hour. If he jackknifed her trailer onto the highway...

She didn't want to contemplate what the consequences might be.

Garth took the truck back two hundred feet, his eyes watching the trailer and traffic, his well-trained ear listening for any and every sound. When the trailer began to veer off a straight line, he stopped and shifted into first. Reversing his procedure, he moved forward, still listening. He pulled up behind his tow truck, a satisfied look on his face. "Timing's off, but your main problem's a bad wheel-bearing," he stated, climbing out of the cab. "Front right wheel."

"I know that!" Dana's dark brown eyes flashed her irritation. He hadn't needed to put her horse in danger just to show off his mechanical expertise. She'd done enough maintenance on the old Ford to be able to diagnose something as basic as a bad wheel-bearing.

"I can't fix it here. I'll have to tow you into the garage."

"But you can fix it tonight?" Again she crossed her fingers. It was after eight o'clock. When she'd called he'd told her the garage was closed, but she'd finally talked him into coming out to look at her truck. She didn't want to have to wait until morning for the repairs to be made and she didn't know of any other place in Kalamazoo to call on a Friday night.

Garth ran his fingers through his hair, staring at the old pickup. He'd really hoped it would be something minor, something he could fix on the spot. On the other hand, it could have been worse. Reluctantly he shrugged. "I guess

I can fix it tonight." He started for the back of her truck. "I'll just unhitch the horse trailer, then put her up."

"Unhitch the—" Dana moved quickly, getting between him and the trailer hitch before he could put his words into action. "We can't leave my horse here. Not on the side of the highway."

"It'll only be for an hour or so."

"No. An hour or so's too long." Any amount of time would be too long. She'd hated leaving her horse while she went to find a phone. She wasn't about to leave him again and chance having him hurt.

Garth looked into eyes so dark they were almost black. Her slender body was blocking his way, her mouth was set in determination. Over the phone, nearly in tears, she'd begged for his help; now she was telling him what he could or couldn't do. If he were smart, he'd just say goodbye and leave. Another twenty minutes and he'd be finished with his car, then he could go home and watch the end of the Tigers game. Here he was facing at least a fifteen-minute tow, plus no less than a half-hour job.

"Please," she said softly.

She was a pretty thing, not much taller than five foot five, he'd guess, the top of her head coming to just below his nose. She looked barely twenty, her reddish-brown hair casually pulled back in a ponytail and no makeup covering her smooth skin. Her only concession to beauty products appeared to be pink lipstick, which she'd already partially chewed off.

With a quick glance he noted she was rather flat chested, had a narrow waist and nice hips. A yellow T-shirt was tucked into a snug-fitting pair of jeans, and scuffed cowboy boots covered her feet. The word *cowgirl* popped into his mind.

His gaze returned to her face. Dammit all, he'd always been a sucker for a damsel in distress. Once again his fingers went through his hair, and he gave in with a sigh. "I suppose I can pull the horse trailer, too."

"Thank you." Slowly Dana let out the breath she'd been holding.

She knew she was asking a lot, but she was desperate. Over two hundred miles separated her from a possible five hundred dollars in prize money. With the cost of a tow and repairs hanging over her head, she needed that money more than ever. "Is there anything I can do to help?"

He shook his head. "Just stay out of my way."

Dana did, stepping as far back from the highway as she could. The passing cars made her nervous. Occasionally she heard Windrunner stomp, but she knew he was all right, just bothered by flies. He was a seasoned traveler, used to long hours in a trailer.

Garth now wasted no motion, his actions swift and precise, his attention on the job at hand. She watched, her eyes following his lithe movements. The man was strong and capable. She had a habit of comparing people to horses. With this compact, muscular mechanic, the quarter horse seemed to fit—the working breed. And like the quarter horse, the man appeared alert, intelligent and quick.

Dana was certain most women would find him attractive. She did. She liked the healthy luster of his rumpled dark brown hair and the way his features were a combination of soft and hard. His nose and lips looked as though they'd been sculpted in clay; yet the strong lines of his jaw and chin made her think of granite. And his eyes were beautiful. A smoky blue, they were framed with lashes so long and lush, she envied him. She tried to figure his age. Early thirties, she decided.

When he had the truck securely attached, he checked the hitch on the trailer, then motioned for her to get into his truck. "So far, so good," he said as he eased out into the traffic, his eyes on his side-view mirror. "Looks like everyone's with us."

Glancing back herself, Dana saw the nose of her truck and the top of the horse trailer. Both looked all right. "Is the garage very far from here?"

"Not far. We should be there by midnight."

"Midnight!" She'd called and told Anne she'd be at her place by ten o'clock. Having found a garage that would help, she was sure she'd be on the road again by nine. Changing a wheel bearing wasn't that big a job.

Dana noticed his smile and stopped fretting. He was obviously exaggerating, and it was better to be slow and safe than to jeopardize her horse's safety. If she was going to be late, she'd just call Anne again. There was little else she could do. She was at the mercy of this man now.

Leaning back in the seat, she studied him more closely. His eyes were on the road, both hands on the steering wheel. Nice hands. His fingers were long and slender, dark smudges of grease caught in his knuckles and under his nails, and his right ring finger showed a band of lighter skin. *He wears a ring.* Almost without realizing it, she checked his left hand for signs of a wedding band. There were none. He was unmarried, or if married, he wasn't advertising it.

From his hands her gaze moved along hair-covered forearms to well-developed biceps and triceps. *A woman could feel secure embraced by those arms.* That thought surprised her. She wasn't one to look to a man for security, and she wasn't one to jump to conclusions. Nevertheless she found herself making other assumptions.

He was a hard worker, sympathetic to others' needs, and a worrier. His grease-stained coveralls and the late hour seemed to support her first conjecture; that he'd come to her aid and had agreed to tow the horse trailer as well as her truck confirmed the second, and the beginnings of worry lines across his forehead hinted at the last.

Probably quite the ladies' man. She'd been aware of his earlier assessment of her figure, when those smoky blue eyes had moved quickly from her head to her toes. He hadn't seemed overly impressed, but that didn't bother her. She wasn't trying to impress anyone with her looks tonight. All she wanted to do was to get to Anne's place. Once there, she wouldn't need to worry about the worn condition of her truck; they were taking Anne's pickup and horse trailer on to St. Charles.

"Do I pass?"

The sound of his voice caught her by surprise and suddenly she realized she'd been staring at him. She certainly couldn't deny it. With an impish grin, Dana answered. "Yeah, you're not too bad-looking."

He laughed, the deep rumble of his voice filling the cab. "Not too bad, huh? Well, you're kinda cute, yourself."

She snorted and faced forward. *Cute.* Gads, how she hated that word. Babies were cute. Puppies and kittens were cute. Women were supposed to be pretty... beautiful... provocative.

A glance down at her hands ended her mental tirade. Her nails were short and ragged, the rose-colored polish chipped. She'd planned to redo them before she left tonight but hadn't had time. From the moment her boss had asked her to work overtime, she'd been running late. Considering the hurried way she'd showered and dressed and that she hadn't even bothered to put on any makeup, perhaps she should be glad he'd used the word *cute*. He might have said "a mess."

From the corner of his eye, Garth watched her. She had a nice forehead, wispy bangs curling toward her eyes. Her nose curved slightly upward. Pert, he'd call it. Even with most of her lipstick chewed off, her mouth was surprisingly alluring. It was ridiculous, she was far too young for him, but he actually had an urge to kiss those lips. What he needed to do was to get his mind on something else. "Where you headed?"

"A friend's tonight, then on to the St. Charles rodeo tomorrow. That's in Illinois . . . west of Chicago."

"I know where St. Charles is. This friend male or female?" It was a nosy question, but he was curious.

"Female. Anne's also a barrel racer. We're buddying up this trip." Dana had to smile. The guy was definitely checking out the territory. She must not look too bad.

"And do you and your friend do this often . . . I mean, race around barrels?"

"I compete just about every weekend. As for Anne . . . well, maybe I shouldn't have used the word *friend* to describe her. We really don't know each other that well and this is the first time we've ever teamed up. She only goes to a few rodeos during the summer."

Garth couldn't remember ever going to a rodeo, couldn't remember even seeing one on television. Baseball and football were his sports. "Barrel racing pay well?"

Dana shrugged. "Anywhere from fifty dollars to a thousand a show. That is, if I place. If I have a bad run, I get nothing."

That was similar to his days of motorcycle racing. "So which has it been—good or bad runs?"

Dana remembered many a weekend in the past when she'd come home empty-handed. It seemed nice to be able to boast about her present standing. "Good ones. Right now I'm tied for first place in the International Professional Rodeo's northeast region. And I'm seventh at the national level."

He could understand her pride. It was a great feeling to be a winner. "When's the championship decided?"

"We accumulate points until mid-September, then at the end of October the Northeast Regional Finals are held in Detroit. Nationals aren't held until January. What's so great is this year, Primo Feed's awarding twenty thousand dollars and the use of a brand-new truck to each regional winner." She desperately needed the truck, and her parents needed every penny of the money.

Garth whistled and hit the blinker for the turnoff he wanted. "Sounds good to me. Maybe I'll take up barrel racing."

Dana's laugh was light and spontaneous. "I think you might have a little trouble with that. Barrel racing is done by women *only*."

Garth found the sound of her laughter a delight. This job was turning into a more enjoyable chore than he'd anticipated. It was nice to be around someone who clearly loved what she was doing. In some ways she reminded him of himself at her age. At twenty, he'd been cocksure on a bike. Then, at twenty-two, he'd hit a wall. The memory made him flinch. "You ever been hurt?"

Staring out the truck window at the neon signs that edged the busy street, Dana remembered Windrunner slipping and falling, the ground coming at her and then the pain. The muscles in her right leg tightened, and she absently began to rotate her foot. "I broke my ankle last year."

He saw the movement of her foot and wondered if her ankle still hurt. She hadn't limped when she walked; in fact she'd had a very nice walk, with just a slight wiggle to her behind. "You're all right now?"

"I'm fine." She glanced his way and smiled. He actually sounded concerned. "Fit as a fiddle and ready to take on the competition . . . that is, assuming I can get to the competition."

"Oh, you'll make it. It won't take long to get that bearing changed."

His words made her feel better. "You know, you were the eighth garage I called. All I got with the others were answering services or the runaround. I could have called my folks, but Dad's truck is in worse shape than mine and never could have pulled the trailer with Windrunner in it."

Garth looked her way. "Where do you live?"

"Just outside of Clay."

Clay, Michigan, was only twenty-five miles from Kalamazoo. Less than that from his apartment. Here he'd thought she was simply passing through; instead, they were practically neighbors.

Not that it mattered, he assured himself and turned off the street onto a paved drive that led to a parking lot and a long metal building. This woman was barely more than a child. Perhaps not naive—he doubted many girls nowadays made it to their twenties as virgins—but definitely too young for a man who'd just celebrated his thirty-second birthday.

On the street end of the building there was a small office with a plastic sign by the door. Dana read it. Roberts's Auto Center. Hours: 8:00 a.m. - 5:00 p.m., Monday through Friday. Closed Saturdays.

So the garage had been closed, and if he hadn't agreed to do the work tonight, she might have been stuck until Monday. That would have been a mess.

Beyond the office a garage door tall enough for a semi to pass through was closed, and farther down the building two normal-size garage doors were also closed. Chain-link fence surrounded the entire area, the only entry being through a massive gate that was now open to allow their passage. A few cars and trucks were parked in the lot—work completed or work to be done, she assumed. The building and lot appeared to be first-class. Picking a name out of a telephone book, she hadn't known what to expect.

"I'll have to unhitch the trailer here," Garth stated, backing the truck so the horse trailer was in one corner of the lot. "That is, if it's all right with you."

Dana knew he was referring to her earlier refusal to leave the trailer by the side of the highway. There, she'd had a few anxious moments waiting for him to make up his mind. Here in this lot, her horse would be safe. "That's fine. While you're working on the truck, I'll walk Windrunner around a little."

Garth watched her back a sleek reddish-brown horse with a white blaze out of the trailer's stall. Even knowing nothing about horses, he was impressed by the muscular development of this one. The short-backed, deep-chested animal was built for speed.

The horse stopped as soon as all four hooves hit the pavement, his dark chocolate eyes showing some white, his small ears perked forward and his nostrils slightly flared. Without moving an inch, the animal looked toward the busy street, then swung his head to face the row of cars along the fence. Finally Dana urged Windrunner toward the cars, speaking to him softly and giving him a chance to get accustomed to his new surroundings. The clatter of his shoes on the pavement echoed off the metal building. Windrunner nickered, then shook his head as the sound bounced back.

"Nobody here but us, boy," Dana said softly, and brushed his tousled mane into place.

Leaning against the trailer, Garth watched Dana's ponytail bounce with each step she took, her hips swaying provocatively. With her slender physique, she hardly looked capable of handling half a ton of horse, yet she seemed in complete control. He envied the animal. It had been a while since he'd had a woman murmur sweet nothings in his ear or run her fingers through his hair. Too long, he decided, and pushed himself away from the trailer. Dana Allen was here to get her truck fixed, not to be ogled by a horny old man. It was time to get to work. "I'm going to move the trucks," he yelled in warning.

Dana took a firmer hold on Windrunner's rope, in case the horse was spooked by the truck starting up, but she wasn't overly concerned. Rodeos presented just about every noise conceivable. The gelding was used to cars and trucks moving about. As her pickup was installed in the garage, she nonchalantly wandered toward the street side of the paved lot.

Although she'd gone to college in Kalamazoo, she'd never been in this part of town before. A multitude of businesses lined the busy thoroughfare, and even at eight-thirty at night, there was a steady flow of traffic. On one side of the garage was an auto-parts store: Roberts's Auto Center. It was set outside the chain-link fence, but was obviously a part of the same company. Hoffman's Swimming Pools was on the other side of the parking lot. A dip in a pool sounded good. It was always hot and humid by the middle of July. Dana fanned herself with the frayed end of the lead rope, and Windrunner whisked his tail at a fly.

After ten minutes of walking, she tied the gelding to the trailer, checked the travel bandages that covered his legs from below his knees to above his black hooves, then began rubbing him down with fly dope. She'd gone over him once before leaving the farm, but she'd been in a hurry then. Now she took her time.

Garth came out of the garage, wiping his hands on a rag. "I've got to go next door and get some wheel-bearings," he yelled. "You all right?"

"Fine," she shouted back and watched him sprint the short distance to the auto-parts store. *Great bod*, she silently admired, then turned her attention back to her horse.

The store was closed, but Garth let himself in with a key. A few minutes later he jogged back, two boxes in his hands.

When Windrunner was rubbed down and completely at ease in his new surroundings, Dana decided to see how her truck was doing. Wiping her hands on the sides of her jeans to remove the oily residue of the fly dope, she sauntered into the garage. From a radio in the corner of the building came a baseball announcer's voice. "Bottom of the fifth, Tigers . . ."

The old blue Ford was up on a hydraulic lift, the right front wheel at eye level to Garth. "How's it going?" she called to him.

"You nearly welded this thing to the axle. Good thing you stopped when you did," he grunted, pulling on a wrench attached to a bearing puller.

"I'd have stopped sooner, but I had the radio on and didn't hear the grinding right away." She didn't admit another reason she didn't hear it was she'd been singing along with Crystal Gayle, albeit off-key.

"Didn't you feel it?" His bulging biceps were enhanced by a sheen of sweat, his grease-covered hands tightening on the handle of the wrench.

She shook her head. "With this old truck, it's hard to tell when there's a problem. The steering wheel has a perpetual shimmy."

At last the wrench moved. Another turn and the bearing popped over the end of the spindle. "Finally." Garth sighed in relief and stepped back for a breather, rubbing his arm across his forehead to wipe away beads of sweat. "That one was a dilly."

He looked her way and smiled, and Dana felt a flutter in the pit of her stomach and an increase in her heart rate. Surprised, she licked dry lips and looked away.

Well, one thing was for certain: she was over John. If a smile from an auto mechanic could set her pulse racing, time had done its job. Once the mortgage on the farm was taken care of, she'd start dating again. Only this time, she'd make certain the man she fell in love with shared her interests. Dana glanced back at Garth and found him watching her.

He was surprised by how she entranced him. Damn, but she was cute. Pretty sharp, too. At least she could recognize a bad wheel-bearing when she heard it. That was more than most women could manage. Usually when one called, she'd say she heard a funny noise, or her car just didn't feel right. Once again he let his eyes travel from the top of Dana's head to the toes of her boots. This time he checked her left hand for an engagement or wedding ring. Her fingers were bare.

She could read the interest in his gaze and had to admit it was flattering. Nevertheless she knew she had to keep her mind on more pressing matters. "Will it take you much longer to fix the wheel?"

Garth returned to the greasy hub. "I'll have this done in a jiff. You get your horse all taken care of?"

"He's been exercised and rubbed down. The flies were bothering him."

"They're bad this year."

"On the farm it's a never-ending battle."

"You always lived in Clay?" Garth reached for the boxes of bearings he'd gotten from the store.

"Except for two years I lived in Battle Creek." Two years she'd shared John Burton's apartment, his bed and his life. "I always felt penned-in there. Guess I'm just a country gal."

"I'm a city boy, myself." With a few taps of his hammer, he set the inner bearing into place. "I don't think I'd know one end of a cow from the other."

"From the udder."

He looked up. "What?"

"Never mind, dumb joke." Dana glanced around the garage. "This looks like a nice place to work. You been here long?"

Her back to him, she didn't see his grin. "Since the place opened."

In the spot next to her truck was a classy white convertible, hood up, its body gleaming and its engine shiny and clean. She stepped over to give it a closer inspection. "Nice car."

"That's my baby," he said proudly, pausing in his work to gaze at his prize possession. "Nineteen fifty-six Ford Thunderbird. As good a car today as it was the day it came off the assembly line."

A classic. Leisurely she strolled around the car. No rust, no dents, everything polished and clean. Even the interior was spotless. Although her truck was always a mess, she could appreciate perfection. "It's a beauty."

"Thank you. I think so, myself. You interested in old cars?"

"Not really. Or old trucks, though it seems to be all we can afford." Hooking her thumbs in her pockets, Dana wandered around the garage. "Boy, my dad would love to have this equipment. There's always something going wrong with the tractor or trucks. If it's not a wheel-bearing, it's the engine." She ambled back, her eyes on the rusted fender near Garth's head. "One of these days this old thing's going to fall apart around me."

"It definitely needs a tune-up. I could do it for you to-night." He wasn't sure why he'd made the offer. Perhaps because, as foolish as it was, he wanted to keep her around for a little while longer.

Dana stopped and looked at him. A tune-up meant money...money she didn't have to spare. The engine was running a little rough, but it would just have to wait until she could buy the parts and do the work herself. "Thanks, but I don't have time tonight. Anne's expecting me. As it is, I'm going to be later than I'd thought."

Garth persisted. "Give her a call and let her know what's up. I've got everything you need here. It wouldn't take me long to change the points and plugs and put in a new con-denser."

As much as she'd like to think it was her, personally, he wanted to keep around for a while longer, she was too practical to hold to such delusions. He was making the of-fer to drum up business; Roberts's Auto Center had a good salesman. The problem was, he was applying his sales pitch to the wrong person. "No, not tonight."

"Maybe next week sometime, then?"

Darn it all, he was making it hard for her to refuse gracefully. Now she had to come up with another excuse. "I work during the day, then have to get home to exercise Windrunner and help my folks. I'm afraid I don't have a minute to spare."

"If you work here in Kalamazoo, maybe I could do it during your lunch hour."

"I work in Battle Creek." She hoped that would dissuade him. Eighteen miles separated the two cities. He certainly should understand that she couldn't simply drive over at lunchtime.

In a few more months he'd have a shop open in Battle Creek, but that wouldn't help him now, and it seemed the more reasons she gave why he couldn't work on her truck, the more he wanted to. "Maybe you could stop on your way back from St. Charles."

"Garth—" She hesitated, her eyes flitting to the name stitched on his chest, then back to his face. "Your name is Garth, isn't it?"

He nodded.

"Garth, to be honest, I can't afford a tune-up. I really can't even afford tonight's bill. Not that you won't get paid," she hurried to assure him. "I do have money set aside for emergencies."

Furrows of concern creased his forehead. "I thought you said you were winning."

"I am." She sighed, wishing the purses were higher and that she had the championship securely tied up. "It's just that I need a lot of money right now."

His eyebrows rose and he waited for her to explain. When Dana didn't go on, he pursued the matter. "Like how much is a lot?"

"Twenty thousand." That would get the bank off their backs.

He whistled at the amount. "That's quite a bundle. And why does one so young need so much money?"

"One so young?" Dana laughed at the comment. "I'm twenty-seven. Hardly a child."

"You're kidding." Twenty-one was the oldest he would have guessed. The attraction he'd felt had bothered him; now he was relieved to know she was only five years his junior.

"I wish I was kidding. I turned twenty-seven last May, while the gal who's tied with me for the championship is only fourteen. I feel like an old lady compared to her. The kid's fearless."

Garth remembered himself at fourteen. He'd been a daredevil, angry at the world and ready to take on anyone and anything. It had taken the accident to show him he was mortal. "You still haven't told me why you need twenty thousand dollars."

He was persistent, she'd give him that. "To help my parents. How much longer before you'll be finished?"

It was clear she didn't want to talk about her need for money. Garth decided to let the subject drop, at least for the moment. He also decided most of this repair job would be on the house. Deftly he pushed a cotter pin into place. "All done."

Now she could leave. But he didn't want her to leave. Turning away from the wheel, he reached for a rag and began to wipe the grease from his hands. "How about joining me for a cup of coffee before you hit the road?"

When he faced her, Dana looked directly into the gray-blue of his eyes, and for a second, considered accepting his invitation. The guy was courteous, good-looking, and it had been a long time since she'd been out on a date, even just a coffee date. Maybe—

Dana stopped herself. It would be silly to start something that couldn't be finished. "Thanks for the invite, Garth, but I can't."

He shrugged and casually tossed the greasy rag into a barrel. "Okay. It was just an idea."

A worthless idea, it seemed. The lady wasn't interested. No big deal. He'd been turned down before. As they always said, there were other fish in the sea. With the push of a button, he brought her truck down. "There she be, ready to go again. If you'll untie your horse, I'll hitch up the trailer."

Ten minutes later the trailer was hitched to the pickup, Windrunner was loaded and Garth stood beside her. "I hope you'll take a check," Dana said, reaching into her truck for her purse. If he said no, they were in real trouble. The only plastic she carried was a gas credit card, and for safety's sake she always kept a minimum of cash on hand.

"A check's fine." He watched her fish through the clutter of items in her purse. It always amazed him how much a woman could cram into such a small space.

Finally she found her checkbook and pen. "How much do I owe you?"

"Fifteen dollars will cover it."

"Fifteen dollars?" Dumbfounded, she gaped at him. She'd estimated the cost of the tow, parts and labor at close to eighty dollars and wouldn't have been surprised—considering the hour—if he'd asked for far more.

"You can afford that, can't you?"

Quickly she closed her mouth. "Of course, I can. It's just . . . that is . . . I'd . . . I'd expected it to be more."

"Well, if you want to give me more, I'll take it." He grinned teasingly. He'd never known any of his customers to pay more than what was asked.

Suddenly Dana understood and frowned. He'd been eyeing her since they met, had asked her out for coffee; some men seemed to feel it their right to barter with sex. Angry, she shook her head. "Forget it, mister, I don't make trades."

His grin widened. He hadn't thought of that. Must be he was getting old. "I'm not asking for anything in return. The fifteen will cover parts and gas. Consider the rest on the house."

Dark eyes searched his face suspiciously. "Why?"

Nonchalantly he leaned against her truck. "I guess I'm just a sucker for cute barrel racers."

"*Cute.*" She winced at the word. "Won't your boss be upset?"

The idea amused him. "Not in the least bit."

"And all you want is fifteen dollars?"

"That's all."

"Okay." Dana filled in that amount. She wasn't going to look a gift horse in the mouth. Every little bit helped.

When she handed him the check, Garth glanced at the upper left corner. It was a custom-printed check, with her address in black against a background of pale blue.

He knew that Clay was a small community, the town consisting of a handful of businesses, a bank and a post office. The surrounding township was primarily rural. Having her house number and the street she lived on, she'd be easy to find. Not that he'd be looking for her, he reminded himself. She'd clearly indicated she wasn't interested.

Dana slipped her checkbook and pen back into her purse. It was time to leave. So what if she wouldn't see him again. In her lifetime she'd met a lot of people she never saw a second time. Still, she hated the idea of leaving. She'd enjoyed the time spent with him. Under other circumstances she might have enjoyed getting to know him better. Almost reluctantly, she shut her purse.

"Well, I guess this is goodbye. I really appreciate what you did for me tonight . . . towing my trailer as well as my truck . . . working overtime. . . ." She shifted her weight and gazed into the depths of his eyes. The words weren't coming easily. "I really don't know what to say. Thank you seems so inadequate."

She held out her hand to shake his, and he looked at her long slender fingers. A handshake seemed equally inadequate. Slowly a smile curved his lips. What the heck. Chances were he'd never see her again. He wasn't after a trade, but he might as well get something for missing most of a Tigers game.

Before Dana realized what he was doing, Garth had straightened his body, placed his hands on her shoulders and was pulling her close. Her lips parting, she started to say something, then the words were cut off as his mouth covered hers.

Warm. Soft. That was how his lips felt. If his kiss had been forceful, she might have pulled back—fought him—but it was gentle and persuasive and Dana found nothing to fight, nothing to run from, only pleasure. Her blood went singing through her arteries, warming her body and weakening her limbs. Her pulse doubled and her heartbeat grew erratic. And then it was over. Just as quickly as it had started, it ended, and Garth stepped back.

"Your thank-you has been accepted," he said, his voice husky. He'd meant to enjoy a simple kiss, satisfy his curiosity and maybe surprise her a little, but it was the unsteady beat of his own heart that was surprising him.

"Garth?" Her legs felt rubbery, and she put out a hand to touch the side of her truck for support.

"Think maybe you'd like to have that cup of coffee some other time?" Her lack of resistance and the dazed look in her eyes gave him hope.

The idea was tempting. Oh, so tempting. "Maybe—" She stopped herself. There were three people depending on her, three people she couldn't let down. Reluctantly

Dana shook her head. "I can't, Garth. I'd like to...believe me, I would. But I can't. The only thing I have time for right now is barrel racing."

"So this is it? Hello, goodbye?"

"This is it." Impulsively she rose to her toes and gave him a quick kiss on the mouth. Then, before he could react, she turned away and swung up behind the wheel. "Bye, Garth. And thanks again."

"Dana?" He took a step closer.

"See ya." She grinned, closed her door and started the pickup.

As she drove out of the lot, Dana glanced into her side-view mirror and saw Garth run his fingers through his unruly hair. He looked stunned. Well, she couldn't say she was exactly uneffected. It had been ages since a man's kiss had affected her this way. For the first time that day, she felt totally alive and ready to take on the world.

"Yahoo!" Dana hooted, honking her horn and heading for the highway.

2

THE CHUTE OPENED and a half ton of brown fury exploded out. Horse and rider hung suspended in midair. All eyes focused on them. Right hand gripping the rigging strap, the cowboy on board brought his heels over the break of the horse's shoulders and leaned as far back as he could. Spurs made contact, turf and hooves met and the dust flew. The cowboy's hat hit the ground, but he was still on.

Then, like a spring, the horse rose into the air again, swapped ends and tried another bone-jarring jump. Knees jerking up and down like piston rods, the cowboy stroked the horse's shoulders, never missing a lick. Fingers crossed, Dana silently counted off the time. One thousand one. One thousand two.

Cody Wright had style, and style was what impressed audiences and judges. Give him a weak horse and he could make it look five points better, stouter. Seven years of competition had turned him from Rookie of the Year to two-time World Champion Bareback Bronc Rider. He was the best, and his wife, Sharon, was Dana's closest friend. From the outside of the ring, the two women watched— one dark-haired and slender, the other blond, petite and seven months pregnant. Silently the two counted off the seconds.

One thousand seven. One thousand eight. The buzzer was a welcome sound, and Dana heard Sharon's sigh of relief. One of the pickup men came up beside the still-bucking horse, and Cody grabbed the man's waist and swung off. His few seconds of glory were over.

"Let's hear it for a good ride," the announcer urged, and the crowd in the grandstand obliged with applause.

"He made it," Sharon exclaimed, her green eyes moist with tears of joy. Stepping back from the fence, she patted her abdomen. "Your daddy did it, Junior!"

"Looked like a good ride to me." Dana smiled. She was continually amused by Sharon's conversations with her unborn child. Sharon insisted the baby knew what she was saying; Dana wasn't about to argue.

Cody picked up his hat, then slowly walked to the side of the ring. He was a lean man with broad shoulders, his muscles well toned and his legs slightly bowed from so many hours of straddling a horse. Only five feet nine inches tall, he gave the impression of greater height and was looked up to by most of the cowboys on the circuit. At the fence he paused to wait for his score. Glancing through the railing at his wife and Dana, he crossed his fingers in the air. Again Dana crossed her own. If he didn't get a high score, those judges were blind.

The announcer's resonant voice came over the speakers. "Cody Wright on Casswell's Comanche Fury...eighty-four points. Highest score so far, folks. Could be the winning ride today. Next, out of chute six, is . . ."

"That should do it," said Sharon. Leaning forward, she called through the fence to her husband. "Good ride. This heat's killin' me. I've got to get somethin' to drink. Want me to bring you something later?"

Cody shook his head and climbed the railing. From atop he watched the next horse and rider break from the chute.

Sharon looked at Dana. "How 'bout you? Want to go with me?"

"You know me. I'm always ready for a Coke." She'd seen enough of the bronc riding; Cody was a cinch to win.

Together the two women walked away from the arena toward a concession stand. Dana's Stetson shaded her face, and her long dark hair was pulled back in a low ponytail. Occasionally a cloud would block the sun, but it was another stinking hot day. She'd put on her long-sleeved Western shirt that morning when it was cool; now she wished she hadn't. A halter top would have been more comfortable.

At the concession stand Sharon ordered a lemonade and Dana a Coke, then they found a place in the shade to sit. "At last." Sharon sighed in relief and rubbed her legs. "I should go watch Cody in the steer wrestling—he's using a new horse—but I've had it. Whatever you do, Dana, don't get pregnant in the summer."

"Last I heard, it takes a man to get a woman pregnant. The way my life's going, I don't need to worry."

"Haven't met anyone interesting, yet?"

Dana thought about Garth and shrugged. "It wouldn't matter if I did. I don't have time for a man in my life. The only thing I have time for right now is winning the regional championship."

"You'll win. I must have known I wouldn't have a chance against you this year. That's why I got pregnant."

"Sure." Dana knew Sharon and Cody had been trying for some time to have a baby. She also knew if Sharon hadn't had two miscarriages, she'd probably be competing right now. Other women had done it—at least until their growing size interfered with their balance. "Just remember, if I do win, it's because of you."

As a teenager, Dana had competed in the pole-bending and speed-racing events put on by Clay's local horse club, but those had been unsanctioned matches that were run for fun and paid jackpots. Sometimes she'd won; more often, she hadn't even placed. Her old quarter horse, HoJo, simply wasn't fast enough. It wasn't until three years ago, after she and John had broken up and she'd bought Windrunner, that she decided to give professional barrel racing a try.

Windrunner was good, but it was Sharon who'd taught her the right equipment to use, how to get the tight turns and speed, and how to prepare for the unexpected. That a rider like Sharon, who'd been barrel racing since the age of five, would even bother to help a rookie had surprised Dana, but from the day they'd first met, their friendship had blossomed and grown, and Sharon had given freely of her knowledge.

"I took you under my wing 'cause I knew you were good," Sharon confessed. "My pa always said, 'Git to know the competition.' So I did." She laughed at that, then turned sober. "How's your folks doin'? They still havin' money problems?"

"Things seem to be getting worse instead of better." Dana sighed and took a long sip of her Coke. "Just last week Dad received a foreclosure notice from the bank. I spent half a day pleading our case."

"And?" Sharon knew the difficulties Dana was facing.

"They finally agreed to give us until November fifteenth to bring the payments up to date."

"It's going to be right down to the line, isn't it?"

"And a lot can happen between now and the regional finals." It worried Dana. A broken ankle this season would be disastrous; yet, she couldn't afford to be cautious. The difference between winning and not even placing was measured in hundredths of a second.

"At least Miss Cocky Britches isn't here today. Someone said she has the flu." Sharon didn't like Connie Birch, the fourteen-year-old who was giving Dana so much competition, and Sharon didn't hesitate to say what she thought on any subject. Tilting her head, she studied Dana's face. "Speakin' of the flu, you look tired. I think you're pushing yourself too hard. Hittin' all these rodeos, holding down a full-time job, helping your folks and working with those handicapped kids. Somethin's gonna give, gal. How they doin'?"

"The kids? Great. If I didn't have that mortgage to worry about, I'd keep my schedule down to a few nearby rodeos and spend my weekends working with them."

"If it was me, I'd quit the job."

"I know." Sharon and Cody hit anywhere from a hundred ten to a hundred twenty rodeos a year. They were truly professionals who made their living from rodeoing, but for Dana that was too much traveling. "Believe it or not, I sometimes get tired of driving to three different shows in as many days. And this weekend it seems like everything is going wrong."

"Like?"

"Like not being able to get Friday off, not getting into Sunday's show, having to work over last night, having my truck go kaput twenty-five miles from my house and having Anne change her mind about buddying up with me."

"Anne Maxwell?"

Dana nodded. "The idea was I would spend last night at her place, then this morning we'd drive here together using her truck and trailer. But this morning she changed her mind. Some guy called and asked her out."

"That's going to cost her, but it sounds like Anne." Sharon grunted and changed position. "It must be nice to have so much money you don't worry about forfeiting entry fees. I swear the only reason she barrel races is to be around the cowboys. She's as bad as the buckle bunnies who follow them from rodeo to rodeo." Shaking the ice in her lemonade, she glanced toward the arena. Just beyond the chutes their trucks and campers were parked. "You got your truck fixed all right?"

"Yes, thank goodness. For a while I had my doubts. No one wanted to come out and even look at it. I'd just about resigned myself to spending the weekend on the side of the freeway when I talked one mechanic into helping me."

"For the cost of an arm and a leg. Right?"

Dana remembered the bill and smiled. "Actually, no, though I might have given him both. To use one of your terms, he was a hunk."

"A hunk, eh? Tell me about him." Sharon leaned forward, definitely curious.

"Well, he had hair about the color of Cody's, maybe even a little darker; beautiful blue eyes, sort of a grayish blue; and shoulders—" Dana held her hands apart, exaggerating the width of Garth's shoulders. "Mmm-mmm. I tell you, the guy was gorgeous."

Sharon laughed. "So, was this hunk married?"

"I don't think so. At least, he wasn't wearing a ring...and he asked me to have coffee with him." She didn't mention the kiss. Sharon would have had a field day with that.

"He did?"

"He did." Dana's dark eyes twinkled in amusement. Sharon was always trying to set her up with a man.

Sharon looked hopeful for a second, then grimaced. "Let me guess. You turned him down, right?"

"Right."

"Dana, when are you going to start dating again? Certainly you're over John by now?"

"I'm over him." When she'd first met Sharon, she'd told her about John. She'd had to, in order to explain why she kept refusing the dates the cowboys offered. And for a long time she'd used John as an excuse, but Dana knew from the way she'd reacted to Garth that John no longer had any hold on her heart.

"If you're over John, why didn't you accept a date with this guy?"

"I turned him down because I don't have time for a man. Besides, it's just as well that I did." Dana took another long sip of her Coke.

"Why's that?"

"Because he's city and I'm country. He said so himself. And I know from experience that I don't belong in the city... at least not to live. Those two years I stayed with John, I felt like I was suffocating... neighbors only the thickness of a wall away, windows that looked into some-one else's window."

"Okay, maybe this guy wasn't for you, but you need to start dating...going out. It's not right for a healthy, lovin' woman like you to be alone. You need a man around."

Dana rolled her eyes upward. Sharon never gave up. "You tell me when I'm going to find time to go out."

"Tonight. After the show, go with Cody and me to The Back Corral. You don't have another rodeo to go to. Who knows, you might meet someone interesting."

Dana doubted that. Since John, no man had interested her—at least not until last night. Remembering Garth and his kiss, she smiled, then realized Sharon was waiting for an answer. "Thanks, but I don't think so. I'm not into picking up a man at a bar, and I really should start back tonight. I have to work on the farm books tomorrow."

"Dana, why not relax...have some fun once in a while? Even if you spend the night here in St. Charles, you'll get home in time tomorrow to do those books. We're staying in the motel down the road. A single's cheap, and they still had lots of vacancies when we checked in."

"I don't know. I'll think about it." Dana knew she wouldn't stay—motel rooms, no matter how cheap, weren't in her budget—but there was no use arguing with Sharon. She finished her Coke and crushed the paper cup in her hand. "I'd better go check on Windrunner. See ya later."

DANA DIDN'T BELIEVE her eyes when she saw Garth leaning against her truck. Logic told her it couldn't possibly be him. She had to be hallucinating. Yet the man resting his elbow on her rusted fender had the same dark brown rumpled hair she remembered from the night before, had the same strong chin and sensuous lips. And had shoulders—their muscular width emphasized by a pale blue knit polo shirt—that were, in fact, nearly as wide as she'd demonstrated to Sharon. He looked out of place in his Italian-cut brown slacks and highly polished brown leather shoes. She hoped he watched where he stepped.

The closer she came to her truck, the less she doubted her eyes—especially when Garth nervously ran his fingers through his hair, rumpling it even more, then gave her the same sensuous smile he'd smiled in the garage. Her heart skipped a beat.

"I was hoping you'd be checking on your horse soon," he called. "You haven't raced yet, have you?"

"No. I'm in tonight's show." Dana stopped a few feet in front of Garth. "What are you doing here?"

"I told you, I've never seen a rodeo before."

His gray-blue eyes traveled over her Western outfit: blue Stetson, periwinkle-blue long-sleeved ruffled cotton shirt, tailor-made blue pants and blue leather boots. The lady in blue. He personally liked the color, and it suited her, bringing out the reddish highlights of her chestnut hair and turning her irises almost black. She was wearing makeup today, a smoky blue shadow accenting her wide, expressive eyes. Makeup made her look a little older, but he still found it difficult to believe she was twenty-seven. He'd bet they carded her in bars.

"You drove two hundred miles just to see a rodeo?" Dana didn't believe him.

"Well, I also have a cousin who lives in Chicago. I'll stop by and see him later." He hoped that sounded casual.

He wasn't really certain why he'd come. All he knew was that when Dana drove away from his garage, an empty feeling had settled inside him and images of her face had haunted him through the night. He'd woken at dawn, after getting very little sleep, determined to concentrate on the architect's proposed plans for his new garage. One pot of coffee and two hours later, he'd realized he was thinking more about Dana Allen than garage dimensions or equipment needs. That was when he'd decided he had to see her again. Four hours of nonstop driving, not always within the speed limit, and he was here. And now, so was she. "You say you're not racing until tonight?"

"Seven-o'clock show. Windrunner and I will be in and out of that arena sometime around eight-thirty."

"Eight-thirty," he repeated. His gaze drifted to her lips, and he remembered how they'd felt against his—soft and giving.

Dana saw his eyes go to her mouth and also remembered the kiss they'd shared. A sweet, curling sensation started in her stomach. "Garth, why did you come here? And don't tell me to see a rodeo."

"I came to see you again," he admitted.

"But why?"

"I'm not sure why." The shrug of his shoulders was poignant. "I just knew I had to."

He was being honest. She had to admire him for that. If she were also honest, she might tell him she was glad he'd come, that she'd wanted to see him again. But she couldn't say those words. If she did, she'd be leading him on and that wasn't her nature. So she gave him another truth. "You're wasting your time."

"Why? You're not married, are you?"

"No," she answered, taken off guard by the question.

"Engaged or anything like that?"

"No. I don't have time for anything like that."

"Why not?"

Dana looked away. "Because I'm too busy."

"I'm not married," he supplied freely. "Never have been."

She told herself it didn't matter if he was married, single or divorced. Nevertheless she was glad to know he wasn't.

A roar of laughter rose from the grandstand. "Watch out, M.J., here he comes again," shouted the announcer.

"What's going on in there?" Garth asked. He could feel her pulling away. Perhaps it had been a mistake to come. Maybe he'd completely misread her response to his kiss. He just didn't know.

"It's the clown. He has a routine he does with the announcer between events," Dana explained, letting her gaze drift back to his face.

She should tell him to get lost. That would end the matter, here and now. She should tell him he was a fool, that she wasn't interested.

But she was.

"I didn't know they had clowns at rodeos." He was playing for time, trying to read the message in her dark eyes.

Dana said nothing.

"Do all rodeos have clowns?"

He was persistent . . . and stubborn . . . and a hunk. She nodded and grinned. "They amuse the crowd and keep the bulls from wiping out the cowboys."

Garth decided to give one more try. "Dana, if I buy a ticket, will you sit with me and explain what goes on at a rodeo?"

Quickly she glanced at Windrunner. The horse was asleep on his feet. No need to worry about him for a while. What the heck, she decided. Why not enjoy an afternoon with a good-looking guy? It wasn't as if she were committing herself to a lifetime relationship. When the rodeo was over, she'd send him on his way. "Forget the ticket. Come on with me. I need to watch my competition, and you can see what a rodeo looks like from behind the scenes."

Heading for the arena, she started Garth's education. "Did you know that the rodeo is the only truly American sport? It originated out West. After a roundup, cowboys used to get together and . . ."

SHARON WAS SITTING on the hood of a truck parked near the fence, Cody standing next to her. Both were laughing at the clowns in the ring when Dana and Garth came up. Dana loved Sharon's reaction when she saw Garth. First Sharon checked out his dark brown hair, then his blue eyes, and finally her gaze drifted to his wide shoulders. "Him?" she mouthed, her eyebrows rising in question.

Garth didn't notice; his attention was on the two clowns in the ring who were pretending to be bullfighting a small terrier. The dog dashed between the taller clown's legs, and Garth laughed with the crowd.

Dana answered Sharon's silent question with a nod. "Garth, I'd like you to meet two friends of mine."

He turned to face them.

"This is Cody Wright, the top bareback bronc rider and steer wrestler in the country, and his wife, Sharon, who taught me all I know about barrel racing. Sharon, Cody, this is Garth—" Dana stopped, realizing she didn't have the slightest idea what Garth's last name was.

"Roberts," Garth supplied, and reached over to shake Cody's hand. "Glad to meet you. I know nothing about rodeos, so you'll have to excuse me if I sound dumb, but what's steer wrestling?"

Cody grinned. "Just a little test of determination. I try to convince a steer to lie down, and he tries to convince me to forget the idea."

"It's not quite that simple," Sharon added for Garth's benefit. "In steer wrestling a cowboy jumps off a horse going thirty-five miles an hour to grab the horns of a running steer, stops it and wrestles it to the ground, flat on its side—all in a matter of seconds."

"Doesn't that hurt the steer?"

"Occasionally, but not often. Those babies weigh six-to nine-hundred pounds. It's the cowboy who usually suffers the most. You oughta see the bruises Cody comes home with."

"She should know. This little lady can't keep her hands off my body." Cody reached over and patted his wife's leg, then ducked as she took a playful swipe at him.

Dana wasn't paying attention to the conversation. Her eyes were on Garth. "Roberts?" she repeated.

He looked her way.

"Like in Roberts's Auto Center? Roberts's Garage?"

"Uh-huh," he answered, giving a sly grin.

"Your father's company?"

"Nope."

"Yours?"

"Yep."

"And does the owner of Roberts's Auto Center usually drive a tow truck at night and change wheel-bearings?"

His grin grew bolder. "Only when a persistent lady insists her life depends on it."

"Her life did depend on it. You were a godsend."

The warmth of her expression was the sweet hug he'd been waiting for. Reaching over, he took her hand in his. "Always ready to save a damsel in distress."

The touch of his flesh against hers triggered a tingly sensation throughout her body. Already hot from the afternoon sun, she felt even hotter.

Sharon didn't miss the flush in Dana's cheeks. "You will be staying for tonight's rodeo, won't you, Garth?"

"He can't, he's going to his cousin's," Dana answered for him.

Now he wished he hadn't mentioned his cousin. He looked at her. "I've changed my mind. At least, I won't be going there right away. I want to see you ride."

"Could you stay a while later?" Sharon continued.

"How much later?" He wasn't sure what she was getting at.

"Until midnight or so. We're partying tonight at The Back Corral. Dana's coming. You're welcome, too."

"No," Dana insisted. "I mean, I don't care what you do, Garth, but I'm not going."

She wiggled her fingers free from his grasp. She didn't want to encourage him to expect anything more than a day at the rodeo. She also didn't want to discover why she was acting so strangely around him.

"Why not?" Sharon's gaze moved to Dana, then back to Garth. "She says no now, but I'm trying to talk her into staying. Maybe you can help me. The Back Corral's mostly a bar, but they serve the best barbecued ribs around and usually have a pretty good country-and-western band."

"Damned good ribs," echoed Cody, grinning and patting his flat stomach.

"Dana deserves a break—a little time for fun," Sharon persisted. "She thinks she needs to drive back tonight, but you've seen that truck of hers. It's a miracle she can keep it on the road. If she stayed over, in the morning you could follow her back and make sure she doesn't have any more trouble."

"Did you have more trouble? What happened to the friend you were going to buddy up with?" Garth had noticed only Windrunner was tied to the trailer.

"No problems. Anne simply changed her mind about coming."

Cody scoffed. "Probably found a man closer to home to chase."

"So Dana's all alone," Sharon pointed out, smiling knowingly at Garth.

"Sharon, I'm not staying over and I don't need an escort home."

"Dana Allen, this man's driven two hundred miles to see you. I'm sure he's not going to mind following you home, and the least you can do is show him how cowboys and cowgirls unwind."

Sharon shifted her gaze to Garth. "I'm right, aren't I? Dana told me about you, how you helped her last night and how good-looking you are. Don't let her give you that bunk about not having enough time and how she has to get back to help her folks. She's already doing more than her share of helping. What she needs is some fun of her own."

"Sharon—" If she could have crawled into a hole and pulled it in with her, Dana would have. She knew her cheeks were red, and she felt totally defenseless when she faced Garth. "I *do* need to get back. I do the farm accounts and I'm way behind."

Garth was pleased with what he'd heard. So Dana Allen had been talking about him. That was good. Right now, she was being pushed into a corner and chances were she'd refuse anything put to her. He'd give her some time. Maybe they wouldn't go to The Back Corral, but they'd be going somewhere tonight. He'd bet on it. Reaching over, he patted her arm. "Don't worry about it. I understand."

She was glad he hadn't put up an argument—and a little disappointed. *Make up your mind*, she chided herself, and turned to watch a cowboy come out on a saddle bronc.

THERE WAS A three-hour break between the first and second show. Most of the cowboys and cowgirls who'd been in the first loaded up and pulled out of the parking lot to hit the road for the next rodeo. New rigs pulled in, horses were unloaded, fees paid and hellos exchanged. The majority of the participants knew one another; they'd been competing against each other for months now, hitting the same rodeos, though not always on the same days.

"So, what did you think of it?" Dana asked Garth as they walked back to her truck.

"Interesting. That bull riding was something else. You couldn't pay me enough to get me on one of those animals."

"A ton of trouble." Dana licked her dry lips and realized she hadn't put on any lipstick since morning.

Garth watched the tip of her tongue slide over her lips and wondered if she had any idea how seductive the gesture was—or if she knew what it did to his insides. Gads, how he'd like to kiss her again. He forced himself to think other thoughts. "What do you do until seven?"

"Make sure Win has enough food and water, get something for myself—" she grinned ruefully "—and try to relax."

"You're not?" She looked relaxed.

Dana rocked her hand from side to side. "I'm never relaxed before I go in. They say the butterflies help." Today's were worse than usual, and she had a feeling some were due to Garth's presence.

"I used to get that way before I raced."

She looked at him. "Raced what?"

"Motorcycles."

"You said 'used to.' You don't get butterflies anymore?"

"No, I don't race anymore. I called it quits when I was twenty-two."

"Were you any good?"

"Yeah." At least he was when he put his mind to it. "I won enough to put the down payment on Roberts's Auto Center."

At her trailer, Dana stopped. The garage she'd seen was almost new. "You just recently bought it?" He certainly looked as if he were older than his mid-twenties.

"I signed the bill of sale on the original building and equipment nine years ago, but business has been good, and I found I had to expand. What you saw was built three years ago. I thought that would be it, but I'm now planning on expanding again—Roberts's Auto Center will soon be in Battle Creek."

Nine plus twenty-two. She'd been right. He was in his early thirties. She checked Windrunner's hay supply, then lifted his water bucket out of its holder. "If I've got the money, when your garage opens, I'll bring my truck there for a tune-up."

"You need a tune-up now, not nine months from now. Here, I'll carry that." He took the bucket from her. "Where we going?"

"There's a faucet over there." She pointed toward a fence post.

Garth carried the bucket, and Dana walked beside him. "Where do you work in Battle Creek?" He wondered if it would be anywhere near the land he'd bought.

"Miller Plastics. It's not a very big company. They make things like knobs for radios and handles for coffeepots. I'm the accountant."

He didn't recognize the company, but he'd look it up when he got back. "You make that drive from Clay to Battle Creek and back every day?"

At the faucet he set down the bucket, and she turned on the water. "Every day of the week. I don't mind the drive. Compared to the miles I put on this truck every weekend, it's nothing. And—" she chuckled "—it's twenty-five minutes I can sing duets with Willie Nelson, Conway Twitty and Barbara Mandrell, and no one knows how badly I sing."

Garth recognized the singers' names, though he was more familiar with Huey Lewis, Bruce Springsteen and Madonna. "What about the social events you miss out on? The good restaurants? Movies? Entertainment?"

Dana shrugged indifferently. "I guess I don't need a lot of entertainment. You ever live in the country?"

"Nope." And he couldn't imagine wanting to. So why was he here when there were dozens of women around

Kalamazoo who would be more suitable for him than this cowgirl?

Probably because not one of those dozens interested him. What he was looking for, he wasn't sure, but in the past year he'd even given up looking—until last night.

"Believe me, there's nothing better than the country," Dana insisted, turning off the water.

That, he intended to find out.

3

GARTH STOOD NEXT to Sharon and Cody outside the rodeo arena. So far six cowgirls, one by one, had entered the ring to compete for the barrel-racing prize money. Running full gallop past the electronic timer, each rider had guided her horse around three fifty-five-gallon barrels in a cloverleaf pattern. Then, from the last barrel to the finish line, each had pushed her horse flat out, to again pass in front of the timer and exit the arena.

Fourteen point three two one seconds was the fastest time from the afternoon round, and none of the six cowgirls so far tonight had crossed the line in less than that time. Another one was now in the ring, her ride going well. But as she rounded the last barrel, the tip of her toe hit the metal can. With a dull thud it fell to the ground.

"Fourteen point nine five two. Would have been second place if she hadn't knocked over the barrel. Let's give the little lady a nice round of applause," the announcer called as the cowgirl raced her horse out of the ring.

"Too bad," said Sharon. "It's a five-second penalty for the knockdown. She's riding with her stirrups set too long. Someone should tell her."

"I imagine you will." Cody chuckled and with his elbow nudged Garth in the ribs. "Since she can't be out there competing this year, she's appointed herself mother hen to all."

"I'm not being a mother hen. I just don't want to see the girl get hurt."

Garth hadn't thought of riding a horse as being as dangerous as riding a motorcycle, but seeing the speed these riders attained and the tight turns they made, he'd changed his mind. Suddenly he was worried about Dana. "Do many riders get hurt?"

"Nah," Sharon assured him.

Cody disagreed. "It's not exactly a tea party out there. Horses spook, fall, run into fences. Last year one gal—"

"Cody—" Sharon growled through clenched teeth, her green eyes narrowing in reaction to her husband's insensitivity.

"What happened?" asked Garth.

"She—" Cody looked at his wife.

"Don't look at me. You started it, you finish it."

To Garth, he explained. "Last year a horse ran into a fence, broke its neck and the rider broke her back. She may never walk again."

Garth fully understood the dangers of a broken back. He'd been lucky. In his case the spinal cord hadn't been severed. Others, he knew, didn't fare as well.

"She had no control over that horse," argued Sharon. "She shouldn't have been competing, to begin with."

"Dana was having trouble with her horse," Garth stated.

"Windrunner always gets excited before he goes out."

"But he was so calm, earlier. The cars and trucks around my place didn't even bother him last night. And while he was tied to the trailer, I would have sworn he was asleep on his feet."

Sharon chuckled, grinning. "Probably was. That horse definitely knows how to conserve energy. However, once it's time to go to work, he's ready."

Garth still found the transformation hard to believe. Dana had had her hands full during intermission when all the barrel racers and calf ropers rode around in the ring, warming up their horses. Windrunner had pranced and danced, tried to take the bit and even bucked. By the time they came out and gathered near the gate, the gelding's reddish coat was covered with a shiny sweat, and Garth was exhausted from simply watching. Yet Dana had maintained a look of calm. She'd grinned when she touched the rim of her hat, crossed her fingers and called, "Wish me luck!"

He turned his attention toward the opening the other riders had come through. According to the program Sharon had handed him, Dana should be entering the arena as soon as the competitor now running left.

The cowgirl rode out.

"Next is Dana Allen. This cowgirl is presently tied for the Northeast Regional Finals and is in seventh place in the national ranking," the announcer informed the crowd.

From the speakers, recorded music played. Garth held his breath, waiting for Dana to come through the gate. One second, two, three passed, yet Dana and Windrunner didn't enter the arena.

"She must be having trouble," Sharon muttered.

"Can you see?" Garth wished he'd stayed with her, but Dana had insisted he join Cody and Sharon at the railing. She'd said he'd get a better view. Maybe of the arena, but he couldn't see any sign of her.

He thought he heard Dana's voice, swearing. Then Windrunner came flying into the ring.

"Oh-oh!"

Sharon's gasp turned the tension into a knot in Garth's gut. "What's the matter?" he demanded, his eyes on Dana. Without hesitation, the reddish-brown horse shot for the first barrel.

"Look at her bridle."

The part of the bridle that was normally around the horse's ears had fallen toward Windrunner's nose.

"She's going to lose it," Cody stated solemnly.

"What will she do?" Garth demanded.

Neither Cody nor Sharon answered.

Windrunner shook his head, not missing a stride in his race toward the first barrel, and the bridle fell so it was hanging below his head.

"All she's got is the bit in his mouth," exclaimed Sharon. "If she can keep the reins tight, she may be able to hold it in there."

Windrunner pivoted around the first barrel and headed for the second.

"Why doesn't she stop him?" Garth's heart was lodged in his throat, the knot in his stomach growing tighter as he watched the chestnut gelding charge for the second barrel. Dana was actually leaning forward, urging the horse on.

"Because she wants to win," explained Cody.

"Feels she has to win," added Sharon. "Come on, girl. Easy…easy. Keep those reins tight. Keep that bit in his mouth. Bring him around. That's it…that's the way. Oh, no!"

The entire crowd gasped as Windrunner finished circling the second barrel and spit the bit out of his mouth. Without slowing a step, the horse ran directly toward the third and final barrel. Dana now had no control over the horse. Running flat out, Windrunner was kicking dust into the air, and all Garth could think of were the bucking chutes directly behind the barrel…chutes filled with massive, mean bulls. Without reins, how would she stop? Mentally he could see the horse crashing into the metal gates, Dana's body being flung into space. *Stop, horse, please stop!* he silently prayed.

"Do it . . . do it," Sharon mouthed, her slender fingers gripping the fence railing. "Come on, Windrunner. Do it."

At the barrel Windrunner pivoted to the left, and Dana held on to the saddle horn and swung her weight to help the horse. Flawlessly he made the turn, straightened and headed for the finish line. Dana urged him on, using her crop. At a dead run, Windrunner passed in front of the timer, then automatically slowed and trotted out the gate.

For a split second there was silence, not even the announcer making a sound. Then his voice came over the speakers. "That, ladies and gentlemen, was one helluva ride. Let's hear it for the little lady."

Applause was mixed with shouts and hoots of joy.

Garth felt as though all the blood had been drained from his body, his stomach and throat hurt and tears smarted his eyes. He blinked them back and chewed on his lower lip, embarrassed by the emotions he felt. Fear, joy, pride and exhilaration—they were all there. Never had he seen anything so beautiful as Dana and her horse running toward that finish line.

"If this baby doesn't come right here and now, I won't know why." Sharon sagged against the fence and wiped her arm across her brow. "She did it!"

"You all right?" Cody touched his wife's shoulders, the look on his bronze face betraying his concern.

"Fine, I guess, now that my heart's back where it belongs." Sharon looked up at her husband and grinned. "I learned her well, didn't I?"

"You shore did."

"Time: 13.825. She takes over first place," the announcer called excitedly, and the crowd again roared its approval.

"Let's go find Dana," suggested Sharon.

Garth didn't need any urging.

DANA WAS STANDING beside her horse, slipping the bridle back on Windrunner's head when she saw the three of them. Both Cody and Sharon were beaming; she wasn't sure how to describe Garth's expression. His eyes were locked on her face, his mouth set in a tight line. He didn't look angry, but he didn't look happy, either. Personally, she was ecstatic. Her horse had just run his fastest time yet. The money and points from this show were certain to be hers.

"Whadja think of that run?" Dana asked, checking to see that the headstall was securely back in place. "Think I should run him without a bridle from now on?"

"Do that and they'll start billing you as the contract act for entertainment. What happened?" Sharon stopped in front of Windrunner and reached out to rub his soft muzzle. The horse blew air from his nostrils and lipped her palm, looking for a treat. Finding none, he blew again and turned his head away.

Dana patted her horse's sweaty neck. "You know how antsy he always gets before he goes in. Well, he kept rubbing his head against one of the fence posts and next thing I knew, the earpiece was sliding down to his eyes. I was going to get off and fix it, but when I shifted weight, he took off."

"Rubbed it off." Sharon laughed. "That's another one for the books. I remember the time Charmayne James's horse, Scamper, bumped the wall in the alleyway at the Las Vegas show and broke the Chicago screw on his headstall. Scamper also made most of the run without a bit in his mouth."

"And won," added Cody.

Dana held up crossed fingers.

"You'll win. No one's going to touch that time," Cody assured her with a smile, then looked toward the arena. Another cowgirl was running the pattern.

Dana glanced at Garth. He'd said nothing since arriving with the others. "So, whatja think?" she asked, not sure he even appreciated what Windrunner had done on his own.

"Not exactly a sport for the fainthearted."

"You ought to have seen him, Dana." Sharon was laughing. "He was white as a sheet when you left that ring."

If Garth's face had been white earlier, it now showed a healthy tan. Dana saw no reason for concern. "I was in no danger."

Garth's eyebrows rose. "You call riding a horse at a dead run with no means of control safe?"

"Windrunner knows the pattern. He should, we've practiced it often enough. Actually, that run was a piece of cake."

Garth held back all the dire thoughts that had crossed his mind while watching Dana fly toward the fence. She seemed unperturbed, even proud of what had happened. To be honest, he was proud of her, too. If he weren't afraid she'd slap him across the face, he'd give her the biggest hug and kiss she could imagine.

"Now you've got to stay tonight," insisted Sharon, watching the way Garth's blue eyes were devouring Dana. "You can't let a time like that go by without some sort of celebration."

A celebration did seem to be in order. It wasn't every day her horse ran the pattern in just over thirteen seconds—without a bridle. "I—"

"Come on," urged Sharon. "Even if you leave afterward, stay for dinner."

Dana looked down at her clothes. She'd had them on since leaving Anne's that morning. She felt dirty and sweaty and was sure she smelled like a horse.

Sharon read her mind. "You can take a shower at our place. Can't she, Cody?"

Cody was still watching the arena and listening to the announcer. Without even glancing toward them, he responded automatically. "Sure, honey. No one's done any better than you, Dana."

"It's settled, then." Sharon looked at Garth. "You're staying, too, aren't you?"

It didn't take Garth long to make up his mind. "Sure."

"What about your cousin in Chicago?" Dana asked.

"He'll be there tomorrow."

"Last horse just kicked the can," Cody informed them.

"You did it!" Sharon squealed in delight and gave Dana a hug.

Garth watched enviously.

DANA DROVE HER TRUCK and trailer over to the motel Sharon and Cody were staying in, and Garth followed. To her surprise, he was driving a Bronco II, not the Thunderbird she'd seen in his garage. "No way would I bring that baby to a rodeo," he'd informed her. "Besides the dust, I want to be able to keep my eyes on that car when I park it."

A two-car man. She'd love to be in that position. She'd love to have one decent vehicle to drive. Feeling the steering wheel shimmy in her hands and hearing the engine sputter when she pressed on the gas pedal, she knew the old Ford desperately needed some work. Maybe she could get to it before the next weekend.

She parked at the back of the motel, out of sight of the office. No need to have the manager checking to see if she was registered. She'd take her shower, change, have dinner at The Back Corral, then be on her way home.

Dana threw a little more hay into Windrunner's manger and hung a bucket of water in the stall. The horse would be all right. Crawling into the back of her truck, she searched for her green plaid blouse and green dress pants. She always carried both of her riding outfits with her. Some days she was the cowgirl in blue, others the cowgirl in green. She was backing out from under the truck's cap when her rear end bumped into something.

"Going somewhere?" Garth chuckled, his large hands hugging her hips, guiding her back.

"I thought I was." As soon as Dana's feet hit pavement, she turned to face him, but he didn't move any farther back, and only inches separated their bodies.

"I got a room." He reached for the taupe tote bag she'd pulled out with her. "You know, there's really no need for you to bother your friends. We can share my shower."

Looking up into the smoldering depths of his smoky blue eyes, Dana had a feeling that if she went with Garth, it would be more than a shower they'd be sharing. For a fleeting moment she remembered his kiss the night before and the delightful sensations his lips had triggered. He was a good-looking man, strong and intelligent. Undoubtedly he'd also be a good lover...and it had been a long time since she'd been with a man.

Dragging her eyes away from his, Dana stared at the center of his chest. Dark hairs curled at the neck opening of his shirt. Every inch of him seemed blatantly masculine.

Slowly she took in a deep, settling breath and forced herself to reconsider what she was thinking. First of all, she barely knew him; one-night stands weren't her thing. Second, she wasn't prepared. A few hours of pleasure certainly wouldn't be worth chancing a pregnancy. Her life was complicated enough. She shouldn't even be tempted.

Yet she was.

Looking back up, she reluctantly gave her answer. "Sounds like a great offer, but Sharon's expecting me. Besides, I'll need to use her hair dryer."

He grinned wickedly, his words seductive. "If that's the only problem, I'm sure we could find some way to dry your hair."

How they might dry her hair led to all sorts of erotic thoughts, and a ripple of anticipation flowed through her body, her skin suddenly growing very warm. Nevertheless, Dana shook her head.

"Maybe another time?"

"Maybe," she murmured huskily, her throat incredibly dry.

Garth continued smiling. He could tell she wasn't indifferent to his suggestion. There was a fire in Dana Allen, a fire he intended to fan. He was a patient man. A year in the hospital had taught him that. Later, after dinner and a few drinks, he'd bring her back to the motel. Her answer would be different then. Confident of the outcome of the night, he stepped back. "Which one's Sharon's room?"

ONLY FORTY-FIVE MINUTES from Chicago, situated in the lovely Fox River Valley, St. Charles was a Mecca for vacationers and antique lovers, and once a year it hosted a rodeo. Over fifty restaurants and bars opened their doors every Saturday night, but it was The Back Corral that drew the cowboys and cowgirls.

Shorty Gray, the owner and host of the establishment, was a former rodeo cowboy himself. Barely reaching five feet six inches, his legs bowed from years of riding broncs and bulls, he had piercing gray eyes, a booming voice and no fear of jumping into a fight. He also had a powerful right hook, which a few unruly patrons had met personally. However, fights seldom occurred at The Back Corral.

People came to drink, eat, dance and have fun. Tonight the place was teeming with cowboys and cowgirls. A low-lying cloud of smoke hung over their heads and the restaurant reeked pleasantly of mash Bourbon and beer sprinkled with salt. A band was playing, but only a few couples were dancing. Most of the women—wives, girlfriends and rodeo groupies—had to be content to listen to the men rehash the day's events.

Dana and Garth followed Sharon and Cody inside. As soon as Shorty saw them, he headed in their direction. "Cody Wright, you old son of a gun, I'll be damned but I swear you get uglier every year."

Shorty clasped Cody's hand, pulled him close and thumped his back. Then he pulled away and nodded at Sharon. "Thought you'd be chasing those cans today."

She patted her belly. "Can't. Junior doesn't like to be bounced around."

Shorty chortled. "I can see you've been ridin' more than those broncos, Cody."

Cody just smiled proudly, and Shorty turned his attention to Dana. "Saw you tonight. One of these days ya oughta try it with a bridle. Might help ya git some speed outta that nag."

"Think so?" Dana laughed and touched Garth's sleeve. "Shorty, this is Garth Roberts."

Shorty's eyes raked over Garth, then came back to Dana, an unspoken question in his expression. Few would mistake Garth for a cowboy. Still wearing the pale blue knit polo shirt, brown slacks and leather shoes, he simply didn't have the look.

"Garth's a friend," she answered. "He owns an auto shop in Michigan. Saved my truck from an early grave last night."

Shorty's hand automatically went out to Garth. "Any friend of Dana's is a friend of mine. Welcome to The Back Corral."

Shorty found a table for them in a corner near the dance floor, took their drink orders and sauntered back to the bar. Garth turned to Dana. "You sure a Coke is all you want?"

"Dana's known as The Coco-Cola Kid," Sharon answered and looked at Dana. "I don't think I've ever seen you drink anything harder."

"Once—" Dana could still remember the night "—when I was in high school. I went to a party where there was drinking. Got drunker than a cowboy on the Fourth of July, then sicker than a dog. That's when I decided to leave the booze alone."

"And you haven't had a drink since?" Garth asked, surprised. He'd known women who'd got sick from too much to drink, but that never seemed to stop them from doing it again.

"Not a drop."

He had to smile. So much for plying her with liquor. If he was going to get her into his bed, he was going to have to find another way.

Shorty delivered a pitcher of beer for the men, a lemonade for Sharon and Dana's Coke, recommended the barbecued spareribs, which they all ordered, then once again disappeared into the throng of customers. When the band started to play a slow, mournful ballad, Garth leaned toward Dana. "May I have this dance, ma'am?"

"Shore can."

Only two other couples were on the dance floor, yet Garth wrapped his arms around her as if it were necessary for him to protect her from the crowd. And she didn't mind. It seemed nice to be enveloped by his strength and warmth. She liked the clean, masculine smell of his body and the aroma of soap. He might not have changed clothes, but he'd showered and shaved.

When he'd come down to Cody and Sharon's room, his hair had still been damp and neatly slicked into place, its color almost black. Since then she'd seen him absently run his fingers through it several times, until once again the dark brown locks had a casual, rumpled look.

"You'd make a good steer wrestler," Dana said, feeling the solid power of Garth's shoulders beneath the soft fabric of his polo shirt.

"Think so?" he whispered near her ear.

"Yes." There was a steellike strength in the arms holding her close.

"Hmm. I don't think wrestling steers is what I want to do."

Dana didn't need to ask what he might want to do; the seductive quality of his voice told her. Sharon was always bragging that Cody's physical prowess made him the greatest lover alive. *What would Garth Roberts be like?* she wondered. The question created a longing she wasn't ready to acknowledge.

"Did I tell you how great you looked in the ring tonight?" he asked, making a slight dip.

"No." She licked her lips. His leg touching hers, even briefly, was unnerving.

He eyed the tip of her tongue and smiled. "Let's put it this way; if it'd been up to me, I'd have given you the money even if your horse hadn't been the fastest."

His arms tightened around her, and Dana felt her heart skip off beat. She laughed self-consciously and tried to ignore the sensuous way he was looking at her. "Well, I think if you had, a few cowgirls might have been after your hide."

Actually, the way some of the cowgirls in the bar had looked at Garth when they'd walked to their table, Dana was sure a few of them did want his hide—or something.

"Hmm." He liked having her firm, lithe body against his. Ever since she'd come strolling toward her truck earlier that afternoon, looking prettier than he'd remembered, he'd wanted to hold her like this.

Her breasts teasing his chest, he could imagine how she'd look without any clothes on. The longer he knew her, the more tempting the idea of making love to her became.

The sexual attraction Garth was feeling wasn't one-sided. A mood of eroticism wrapped itself around Dana, engulfing her. The need she'd been feeling refused to go away. Every synchronized dance step they took, every movement of their bodies, added to her growing desire. She found it impossible not to react to the warmth of his breath on her hair, or to keep from inhaling sharply when he reached up and pulled the scarf from her ponytail, making her hair fall in soft waves about her shoulders.

"Nice," he murmured, his voice a husky whisper. "Very nice."

"Garth?" Her heart was beating wildly. Gazing into his eyes, she licked her lips again.

"Yes?" He lowered his head, wanting to taste her mouth.

Dana quickly turned her face and pressed her cheek against his shoulder. She wanted him to kiss her, but she didn't. She was afraid. If he kissed her, she might not be able to control this strange longing.

But he did kiss her. Light as a feather his lips touched the top of her head. And he inhaled the clean scent of her hair and the sweet, very feminine aroma of her body. He wanted her, and he had a feeling—in spite of the turning of her head—that she wanted him. For the time being, he would keep his emotions under control. Now they would eat, drink and be merry, but later—when they were alone—he would discover what made Dana Allen so very special.

4

IT WAS AFTER ONE before Garth drove the Bronco out of The Back Corral's parking lot. Dana hadn't expected to stay this late. Originally she'd planned to drive her truck and trailer over, have dinner, and leave as soon as she finished. But Garth had insisted on taking her, promising to bring her back to the motel whenever she wanted.

The problem was, she'd been having so much fun, she forgot the time. Now she could barely keep her eyes open. The idea of getting into her truck and heading home held no appeal, but she knew she had to. She couldn't afford a motel room. What she'd do was get a start, then pull into a rest stop for a few hours of sleep.

Driving home tired after a weekend of hitting three or four rodeos wasn't anything unusual. Since early spring it had become the pattern of her life. She wished, though, that Anne had come. It was always easier if she had someone to buddy up with, someone to talk to when road fatigue threatened to take over.

Of course if Anne had come, she probably wouldn't have gone to The Back Corral with Garth; probably wouldn't have had as much fun. Through half-closed lids, Dana looked his way.

It seemed impossible she'd known this man less than eighteen hours. He certainly had an effect on her. Dancing with him—being held in his arms—was a combination of ecstasy and torture. Even when they weren't dancing, every time he touched her, her heart took a leap and her pulse went crazy. There'd been times tonight when she'd felt downright giddy, and she was glad she wasn't drinking anything stronger than Coke.

The party at The Back Corral had really been just getting going when she realized how late it was. Cody and Sharon would undoubtedly stay until the bar closed, but for Dana, the time to celebrate had come to an end. Soon she'd be saying good-night to Garth . . . and goodbye.

It wasn't that she didn't like him. She did. Shoot, everyone seemed to like Garth Roberts. Cody hadn't actually come out and said so, but Dana could tell he did, and Sharon, dear Sharon, couldn't wait until she got her alone in the bathroom to go on and on about how fantastic Garth was and that only a fool would let a man like him get away.

Too bad Sharon was wrong.

Dana knew from experience she'd be the fool if she did think there was a future for them. How could there be? They were too different. During dinner Garth had admitted he knew nothing about horses and was even a little afraid of them. His love was cars—old and new. He was involved with his work . . . and he loved living in an apartment.

An apartment. Dana could remember all too well John's apartment, with its paper-thin walls and creaking doors. Why anyone would want to live in the city, fight traffic, breathe contaminated air and have people around all the time was beyond her comprehension. She certainly hadn't enjoyed it. She was a country girl.

And Garth Roberts was a city boy.

It was a shame, but it really didn't matter if he excited her physically, if Cody approved of him, or if Sharon thought she was a fool. Garth and she were simply too

different. Too bad, too. She'd really enjoyed being with
him. Dana sighed in regret.

"Tired?"

She snapped out of her reverie. Garth was looking at
her, his expression concerned. Stifling a yawn, she managed a smile. "A little. It's been a long day."

"What you need is a nice, soft bed." He reached over and
brushed the backs of his fingers along the side of her face.
She was so lovely, with her hair still down around her
shoulders, her skin as smooth as velvet. He could hardly
wait to get to the motel. They'd go to bed, all right, but he
doubted they'd get much sleep—at least, not for a while.

Dana enjoyed the gentle caress of his fingers. It was nice
having a man concerned about her well-being. A bed did
sound delightful. The year before, she would have gotten
a motel room and stayed over. The year before, rodeoing
had been fun; she'd gone when she wanted, stayed over if
she was tired and tried to win because it was a personal
challenge, not a necessity.

What a difference a year made. Barrel racing was now
her second job, not a hobby. She had to win, had to pinch
pennies, had to show a profit each week and had to keep
on going, no matter how she felt. And tonight she felt
tired.

It was still warm out and Garth had the air conditioner
on. The steady hum of the fan was hypnotic. Streetlights
alternated with darkness, then became a blur. Garth was
still caressing her cheek and it felt so good. Her lids
drooped, then closed, and she relaxed against the seat,
giving in to her exhaustion.

He could hear the even rhythm of her breathing and
knew she was asleep. His hand moved back to the steering wheel, and he smiled. She looked so young and in-
nocent, her head tilted to the side, her lashes touching her

cheeks. Her lipstick was gone again—not that it mattered; she looked beautiful without it.

Carefully he turned in at the motel, drove past the office with its No Vacancy sign. When he came to the next-to-last door along a long line of rooms he parked the Bronco.

Back by the fence he could see Dana's truck and horse trailer. Windrunner was in it. She'd said the horse would be fine, that he was used to being in the trailer for long hours. Garth hoped so. What he wanted now was to get Dana into bed—his bed—not exercise a horse.

Even after he turned off the motor, Dana slept. Garth released his seat belt and twisted sideways to look at her. He wasn't one who believed in love at first sight, but he felt something for this woman. *What you want is her body,* his subconscious told him, and he had to grin. Maybe that was all it was. Dana Allen turned him on. Leaning toward her, he let his lips lightly brush over hers.

Dana stirred, automatically returned his kiss, then blinked open her eyes and pulled back slightly. "Oh, I—"

"Hi," he murmured, the smoldering warmth in his eyes relaying the rest of his message.

Dana could feel her abdominal muscles tighten and her pulse increase. Her thoughts were hazy, but she was aware enough to know that Garth was kissing her and she liked it. His lips touched hers again; his hand moved behind her head to bring her closer.

Why not enjoy a kiss? she wondered. She'd probably never see him again. Sharon had said it: she needed to relax and enjoy life. And what better way to do it than by kissing a man like Garth Roberts.

Her senses came alive as her mouth moved with his. She could taste the tangy bitterness of the beer Garth had drunk and smell the lingering hint of soap on his chin.

Without breaking contact, he reached down and released her seat belt, then slipped his arm around her shoulders, drawing her even closer.

For a moment Dana wasn't sure what to do with her hands. They seemed in the way. Then, tentatively, she touched his waist, resting her fingers just above his hips. The heat of his skin radiated out from beneath his shirt. Growing bolder, she moved her hands up over his back to his shoulders. The feel of his muscles excited her.

"Nice," he murmured.

"Uh-hmm," She didn't want to talk. Talking took his lips away from hers and she liked the feel of his mouth.

But Garth did talk, his voice husky. "Ever since I kissed you last night, I've wanted to kiss you again."

"Really?" *It's just a line,* she told herself, but she wanted to believe it. He had, after all, driven a long way to see her.

"Yes, really." He nibbled at the soft skin of her cheek. She even tasted good. "And what about you? Did you want me to kiss you again?"

His lips moved to her earlobe, his tongue dipping in. A tingly rush distracted all thoughts, her breathing became shallow. "I . . . I—"

"Yes?" His laughter was low and throaty. "I think the I's have it." Again his mouth covered hers.

Differences. Suddenly they seemed insignificant. Inconsequential. Delightful. Dana tightened her hold around his back and moved her lips with his in a harmonious exploration. Their breaths blended, their hearts were beating in unison.

The tip of his tongue invaded the inner space of her mouth, and she welcomed the assault. In, out . . . then in again. Each thrust was slow, intimate and deliciously erotic. Her abdominal muscles tightened even more, and between her legs she felt a moist warmth she couldn't control. His hands roamed over her back, and her skin grew hot, then hotter. Breathing ceased to be an easy matter; rational thinking, impossible.

Her breasts were swelling, her nipples growing hard. The rigid nubs pushed against the nylon lace of her bra, straining for release, and she ached for his touch until it was a welcome relief when Garth worked his fingers between their bodies to caress her.

Sitting back a little, he gently stroked one small breast, then the other. "Does that feel good?"

"Yes," she acknowledged, her pulse racing so fast she felt heady.

"Good. I'm glad." He kissed the tip of her nose . . . her cheeks . . . her eyelids. "I want to make you feel good all over." Slowly, one by one, he released the top buttons of her blouse. "I want to get to know you, find out what you like, what makes you happy."

Mesmerized, she didn't stop him. It had been so long since she'd made love, it seemed like a dream, a wonderful fantasy. Even when her blouse fell open and his fingertips found the lacy trim of her bra, she didn't think about saying no. Gently his hand investigated the new territory, his palm rubbing over the silky material, feeling the taut bud beneath, circling it, then rubbing over it again.

Dana groaned in pleasure.

He wanted to free her breasts, look at them, taste them. He wanted to take off all her clothes—and his. His slacks were growing uncomfortably tight, his twisted position not helping the pressure in his groin. "You know, it's silly for us to sit in this car, making out like a couple of teenagers, when we have a perfectly good bed waiting for us just inside."

Bed. The word hit her like a splash of ice water. Suddenly Dana was all too aware of what she was doing and where they were headed. Her dark eyes opened wide. "Garth, I can't. I'm sorry...I...I've got to go."

She tried to pull away, but his arm tightened around her back, holding her close and preventing her from moving. "Dana, what's wrong?" He knew he hadn't misread her signals. She wanted him, just as he wanted her.

"I made a mistake. Things shouldn't have gone this far."

"Things haven't gone far enough." He needed the physical relief she could bring him. "Don't worry, I'll take care of things." He never left that up to chance.

"It's not just that. I...I just can't." Unable to pull free, she stopped fighting and rested her forehead against his shoulder. She tried to get her heartbeat and breathing back to normal. Everything had happened too fast. She should have stopped him long ago.

"Dana, believe me, I don't do this with every woman I meet. Maybe we haven't known each other very long, but I like you—like you a lot." He knew what he was saying sounded like a line, but it was the truth.

She wanted to believe him, yet it didn't matter. A night of making love would complicate her life. Right now, Garth Roberts was an interesting man she'd met, spent time with and kissed. He'd touched her, both physically and mentally, but she was sure she could easily forget him. If they shared a bed, he might not be as easily relegated to the back of her mind. No, she couldn't chance it.

Again she tried to pull back, and this time he let her. Looking him directly in the eye, she tried to explain. "Garth, I'm sorry. I have no intention of sleeping with you. I never did."

"Then why in the hell did you let things go as far as they did?" he demanded. One thing he hated was a woman who was a tease.

Dana wished she had an answer. "I don't know why. Usually I don't let a man even kiss me. Shoot, I haven't even been out on a date for over a year."

"I find that hard to believe." Yet he remembered Sharon saying something about Dana working too hard.

"Well, it's the truth," she flared. She didn't like being called a liar.

He took in a deep breath, then expelled it, his gaze never leaving her face. Maybe she *hadn't* been playing a game. Maybe what had happened had simply happened. Either way, it was obvious she wasn't going to go to bed with him. "Damn!"

"I'm sorry. Really I am." Looking down, Dana chewed on her lower lip.

Another deep breath gave him time to think. "If you don't plan on sleeping with me, then just where are you going to sleep? Sharon and Cody had a single and this place is full."

She didn't even bother to look at the vacancy sign behind her. She was sure he was right. "Nowhere. I'm going to start home."

"Tonight?" He couldn't believe her.

Her head came back up. "Yes. Now."

"You couldn't even keep your eyes open on the way back here."

"I was a little tired when I left the bar—I'll admit that. But I'm fine now." Nothing like a little necking to get the blood circulating and the mind working again, she thought.

"A *little* tired?" he scoffed.

Lifting her chin, she looked him straight in the eye. "I'm fine now. When I get too tired to drive, I'll find a rest stop and take a nap. I've done it lots of times." She was sure she was good for at least fifty miles . . . maybe more.

"You'll do no such thing." He opened his door and got out.

Buttoning her blouse, Dana opened the other door and slid out. Garth walked around the front of the Bronco; she headed for the back. She was two steps away from his car, going toward her truck, when he grabbed her arm. "Don't be ridiculous, Dana. If you don't want to make love, we don't have to make love, but I'm not letting you drive back to Michigan tonight."

She turned to face him, the storm reflected in her eyes about to erupt. "And since when did you become my keeper?"

"Since you stopped showing good sense."

One thing she'd learned from John that she didn't regret was a basic knowledge of self-defense. He'd insisted she learn certain escapes and throws. With a twist and a pull, she had her arm free of Garth's hold and was again on her way toward her truck.

For a second, Garth didn't realize what she'd done. One moment he'd had her, the next he didn't. Staring at her back, he watched her move with a determined step, head held high. Then he hurried to catch up with her.

"All right, I can't make you do anything. But be reasonable, Dana. I've paid for the room, the bed's there. I promise I won't touch you if you don't want me to."

From the corner of her eye, she looked at him, not slowing a step. "If you don't want me to" was the phrase that bothered her. If she were in a room with him, sharing a bed, would she want him to keep his hands off her?

Would she be able to keep her hands off him? She wasn't sure.

He could tell he hadn't convinced her. He had to find another argument. "Dana, you're jeopardizing your horse's life as well as your own."

Pulling out a key, she unlocked her truck door. "I'll stop before I put either of our lives in jeopardy."

"Dana, please . . ." Again he put a hand on her arm.

She looked down at it, then up. "Garth, I'm leaving, and that's that. I will say I had a great time tonight. I enjoyed dinner, you're a great dancer and lots of fun to be around." Rising up on her toes, she pressed a kiss to his lips, then settled back on her heels. "You're also, definitely, a great kisser. Maybe a little crazy, too, driving two hundred miles to see a rodeo. Yes, crazy." She smiled. "But nice."

"I'm going with you," he decided.

She frowned. "Going with me?"

"Yes. If you're so determined to get back to Michigan tonight, we'll go. Give me the key and I'll drive."

"And what about your car?" she asked, nodding toward the Bronco.

Damn! He hadn't thought of that. Two hundred miles was a bit far behind to be leaving his main means of transportation. "All right then, I'll follow you. At least then, if you have any problems, I'll be right behind you. Just give me a few minutes to get my things out of the room."

Dana considered the idea. Garth had shown he was persistent. If she said no, he'd probably hop in the trailer with Windrunner, just to make sure she took him along. "Okay," she agreed, another plan forming in her mind.

She waited until he was in his room before she hopped into her cab and started the truck's engine. Without even looking back, she headed for the main street. She hoped he'd take the hint and forget about following her. Now was the time to end this relationship. He'd probably be madder than hell, but she didn't care.

She was on the freeway before she began to suspect that the headlights directly behind her might belong to Garth's Bronco. At one-thirty in the morning, there wasn't much traffic on the road. She slowed down to see if the vehicle would pass. It didn't. Then she sped up. Again the car stayed the same distance behind. "You idiot," she swore and settled back to a safer speed.

Mile after mile the car followed. Keeping tabs on it helped keep her alert. Around the outskirts of Chicago she drove; the traffic was light, the city asleep. Tolls were paid and the Indiana border was crossed. After a while she turned on the radio and sang. She hoped for Garth's sake that he had his windows rolled up and couldn't hear her.

When her vision began to blur, she looked for a rest stop. The idea of facing Garth again didn't appeal to her, but she knew she couldn't keep going. When she hit her turn signal she wasn't surprised to see the vehicle behind her also flash for a turn. Easing her truck and trailer into a parking spot, she turned off the motor and lights, leaned back against the seat, rubbed tired neck muscles and closed her eyes.

A minute later, her door opened with a jerk. "Are you planning on sleeping in there?"

"No." Dana opened her eyes and forced a smile. Picking up her purse, she slid out past Garth. "Nice driving this time of night, isn't it?"

He grunted, his eyes narrowed as he watched her head for the trailer. Rubbing his own tired neck muscles, he grumbled, "I thought you were never going to stop."

She looked back before going around the end to check on Windrunner. "Hey, I didn't ask you to follow me."

"You didn't even wait."

"I thought you'd take the hint."

"I'm a little thick skulled."

"Obviously." The lights in the parking area illuminated the inside of the trailer. Her horse looked fine. Garth was still standing near her door when she walked back to the rear of her truck. "Look, I'm sorry if I was rude, but I didn't want you to follow me. I thought if I left, you'd just stay where you were."

He said nothing, but his eyes were eloquent. He was furious.

Well, she didn't feel guilty. She hadn't asked him along. She hadn't asked him to come to St. Charles. With the turn of her key, she opened the back of the cab. "Good night, Garth. I'm going to get some sleep."

"What about your door?" he asked.

She realized then that she'd left it open and the ceiling light was still on in the cab. But of course, she'd had to leave it open; he'd been standing in the way. "Would you close it, please?"

"Certainly." He smiled, but the smile didn't go to his eyes. And he didn't move.

Dana shrugged and turned away. She was too tired to argue. Crawling onto the mattress she kept in the back, she wondered if he'd try to sleep with her. She hoped not. She didn't have the energy to fight him off.

Wearily she punched her pillow into place and pulled a light blanket up over her shoulders. The truck rocked a little, and she heard the door being shut. At least he'd done as she'd asked. Closing her eyes, she fell asleep.

THE SUN WAS UP when Dana crawled out of the back of her truck. She yawned, stretched, then headed for the bathrooms. Ten minutes later she came out, a good brushing having brought her tangled hair enough under control for her to put a scarf around it, a little toothpaste having refreshed her mouth and a good scrubbing having brought color to her cheeks.

Windrunner was next. He needed to be walked, watered and fed. She was almost past the cab of her truck, on her way to the trailer, when she suddenly stopped and stared in the side window. "Crazy," she muttered, shaking her head. "The man's absolutely crazy."

Garth was scrunched up on the seat, his body twisted in an odd way, his legs bent. How he could sleep in that position was beyond her, but he was doing it. Lightly she tapped on the window.

He stirred.

"Wake up, sleepyhead," she called through the opening at the top of the window.

Hazy blue eyes met with hers. She could tell he wasn't sure where he was . . . or why. He smacked his lips and ran his tongue over his teeth. Then suddenly he sat up, his eyes widening, and she knew he'd remembered.

"Sorry to bother you, but after I exercise Windrunner, I'll be hitting the road again. Thought you might like to use the bathroom." She grinned and started toward the trailer.

Garth opened the truck door and got out. His back ached from his shoulders to his tailbone. It had been a while since it had given him any trouble. But then, it had been a while since he'd slept in the cab of a truck. Twisting and flexing, he tried to loosen stiff muscles.

Dana backed her horse out of the trailer and walked him toward a grassy patch. Over her shoulder she called back to Garth. "Sleep well?"

"Sure. Great. Nothing quite like a night in a truck." He laughed at himself. He had to be crazy, chasing after this woman. Watching the sway of her hips, he shook his head. No doubt about it, he was crazy. Stiffly he followed her.

Windrunner kept trying to graze as Dana walked him. She couldn't blame the horse. The grass at the rest stop was lush and green. Her stomach grumbled. Breakfast sounded pretty good to her, too.

Garth heard. "Hungry?"

"A little. Considering all those ribs I ate last night, I don't see why."

He glanced at his watch. "It's after eight, that's why. Those ribs are long gone. Where do you want to stop for breakfast?"

"Garth . . ." She shook her head. The guy was unbelievable. She knew if she didn't stop, he wouldn't. And if she did, he would. So why make it difficult. "I know a place in Benton Harbor. Just follow me."

"I intend to." He raised his eyebrows. "Do I dare leave you for a minute?"

Walking away from him, Windrunner by her side, Dana smiled. "We'll be taking our morning stroll for the next fifteen minutes. You can do as you like."

By EIGHT-THIRTY they were on the road again. A little after nine o'clock they were at the restaurant. When Dana pulled her truck and horse trailer into the spacious parking lot, Garth pulled in behind her. "I'm starving," she admitted, stepping out of the truck at the same time he slid out of the Bronco. "In fact, I think I could eat a horse."

Windrunner nickered and Dana laughed, peeking into the back of the trailer to make certain the horse looked all right. "Don't worry, old boy, not you."

"What I need is a cup of coffee," Garth confessed. "I'm worthless in the morning until my first cup."

She gave Windrunner's rump an affectionate pat, then walked with Garth toward the restaurant. "Coffee's another thing I don't drink."

"Just Coke?"

"Just Coke, milk and orange juice." She laughed. "I guess I never grew up."

His eyes skimmed her figure and he smiled, remembering the feel of her body. "Oh, you grew up."

Dana felt her cheeks grow warm and knew she was blushing. How silly. She never blushed. Maybe she was reverting to her childhood. Running out on Garth last night had been a childish thing to do. She'd blame it on exhaustion. Her mind never functioned well after midnight.

Inside they found a table by the window where she could keep an eye on her rig. "I always worry that something might happen to him," she explained. "Although he travels well, you never know with a horse, and I certainly can't afford to have Windrunner hurt."

"Last night Sharon said she thought you could go all the way to the national finals on that horse, that you should quit your job and just rodeo."

"Sharon has a lot of faith in me, but I'm too chicken to quit. For every cowgirl who makes money on the circuit, there are dozens who only break even or lose money. Right now I'm winning, but that could change. With things the way they are at home, I need my job to guarantee the bills are paid."

"If you could, though, would you quit your job and just rodeo?" He wondered what it would be like, spending every weekend going from rodeo to rodeo. He didn't think he'd like it. Not every weekend. Maybe he should try to forget this cowgirl.

If he could.

Dana considered his question for a moment, then shook her head. "No. For one thing, I like my job. Second, for me at least, having to make a living off winning at rodeos takes all the fun out of going. I've noticed that already this year. If I win the regional championship in October, I'll go on to the nationals, but after that I'm cutting back—way back. I've got other things I'd like to do."

"Like what?"

She wasn't sure if he'd understand. Some people didn't. "Like teach the handicapped to ride."

"How handicapped?" The idea interested him.

"Any disability that might make it hard for a person to ride. I especially like working with kids. Right now, I'm teaching a blind boy, a girl who has cerebral palsy and one with Down's syndrome. If I had more time and more horses, I'd take on others. They're out there, and they're so eager to learn." She shrugged, frustrated. "But that's just a dream I have."

"Can't you buy more horses?"

"No." She picked up the menu.

"Why?"

"Because it takes money to buy and keep horses, and right now all the money I can earn has to go to saving the farm." Suddenly she stopped and laughed at herself. "Oh, my, doesn't that sound dramatic! I've got to save the family farm."

It did sound dramatic and like a tall order. "Tell me about it," Garth said.

The waitress came back with Dana's Coke. Setting it down, she pulled out her pad and pencil. "Ready to order?"

Dana was glad for the interruption. "I'll have two eggs over easy, hash browns and whole-wheat toast."

Garth ordered the same, plus sausage. He waited for the waitress to leave, then rephrased his question. "Tell me why your family farm needs saving?"

"It's a long story. You really wouldn't be interested." And it wasn't one she told to many.

"Try me."

"You know, you're a pest." She tried to laugh him off, but the steady look in his eyes told her she wasn't going to succeed.

Staring down at her Coke, she wondered how to explain what had happened—or how it had happened. There were times she blamed herself, times she blamed her father and times she blamed the economy. She guessed she'd start with the economy. "The family farm needs saving because a few years ago money was too easy to come by. The economy was on the upswing, interest rates were low and banks were passing out loans like candy.

"Then the bottom dropped out, commodity prices fell and the farmer could barely break even, much less pay back the large sums of money he'd borrowed. The friendly banker became less friendly, and equipment was repossessed."

"Your father went too far into debt," Garth murmured. It had happened to businessmen he knew.

She nodded. "The corn picker and baler he'd bought on time went back, along with two new silos, but he couldn't return the new roof on the barn or the feeder calves and he needed the tractor. Also, he couldn't return the second mortgage he'd taken out to have the money to send me to college."

Garth said nothing, letting what she'd said sink in.

Dana sighed. "If I'd known that's how he'd gotten the money, I wouldn't have gone to Western, but he said he'd been saving it since I'd been born, and I believed him. If I'd realized any of what Dad was doing, maybe I could have helped."

"When did you find out?"

"Last Christmas." That was a day she'd never forget: her mother crying, her brother sulking because he hadn't gotten the present he'd wanted and her dad trying to minimize the problem. It took a month before he confessed how badly in debt they really were.

"And how bad is it?"

"Bad. I may have a head for numbers, but my dad doesn't." Her father's accounting system was something Dana found hard to understand. "You wouldn't believe the mess he had the farm books in. He used the shoe-box form of accounting. If a bill came in, it went into the box. Then, when he had some money, he'd pay the first ones he pulled out of the box, no matter how recent or overdue they might be, or if payment could have been delayed or spread out. And if he remembered to record anything, it was a miracle."

Garth remembered she was heading home to work on the farm's books. "So you've taken over the bookkeeping."

"At least until this mess with the mortgage is straightened out."

"How far behind are the mortgage payments?"

"How's twenty thousand sound?"

He gave a low whistle.

The waitress brought their food, setting the plates of eggs and hash browns in front of them. Both Garth and Dana stopped talking, waiting for the woman to leave before going on. Finally, with Garth's plate of sausage and the toast on the table and his coffee refilled, they were again alone.

"There's just you and your parents, then?" he asked, picking up a fork.

"Any my brother, Danny."

"Is your brother shouldering this financial responsibility as much as you are?" It seemed to him that Dana was taking on too much.

She grinned and broke up her egg yolks, mixing them with her hash browns. "As much as he can. Danny's only ten years old."

Garth's egg-laden fork stopped midway to his mouth. He hadn't expected her brother to be that young.

She understood. Having a brother seventeen years younger surprised a lot of people. Danny had even surprised her parents. "Mom and Dad didn't think they could have any more children. For years after I was born they tried, unsuccessfully. Then, when my mother was thirty-nine, along came Daniel James Allen the second. He's spoiled rotten and proves everything they say about a kid brother." She paused, gathering the mixture of egg and potatoes onto her fork. "But I love him.

"In a way, I want to save the farm for him. Danny says he wants to be a farmer when he grows up, and I think he will be. Even now he helps Dad with the chores, he's raising twenty calves and he drives the tractor when we bale hay. If we lose the place, it would crush him as well as Dad."

Garth liked her loyalty to her family; yet he was concerned. "Dana, you're asking too much of yourself. Holding down a full-time job and doing the farm bookkeeping is one thing, but traveling hundreds of miles every weekend to put your life on the line in a rodeo arena?"

"I'm not putting my life on the line." She laughed at the idea. "And I'm not asking too much of myself. Don't forget, a portion of that mortgage money went to pay for my college education. I owe Dad."

He wished she didn't. Watching her race her horse dead out around those barrels had bothered him. Knowing she was racing for money, he was sure she'd take chances. He knew he had when he was racing.

As they ate, Garth asked more questions about her family and the farm. She answered them all, told him the twenty thousand Primo Feed was putting up for the Northeast finals winner would easily bring the mortgage payments up to date, but that if she didn't win, on November 15 the bank would foreclose.

"What about the money you won this weekend?" he asked. "Doesn't that help?"

"A little. It's all going into a savings account. I'd love to end up with way too much money in November. But I sure won't if I have many more weekends like this one." She explained. "I should have been at rodeos Friday and today, but by the time Mom called me in, today's competition was filled. And I had to work Friday."

"Called you in?"

"Every Monday or Tuesday, Mom calls the secretaries at several rodeos being put on the following weekend. What she tries to do is get the best dates and times for me, so I can drive from one to the next, hitting as many as possible. The problem is, sometimes they reach their quota before she gets through. In that case, I'm out of luck and out of money."

It was all new to him. "What about yesterday? You did pretty well, didn't you?"

"What I won will pay my expenses plus give Dad a little for the account. But St. Charles didn't pay day money." She didn't wait for him to ask. "That's money that's added to the pot. That way, when there's more than one performance of a rodeo, the winners of each show can take home something, even if their times don't end up being the fastest. The winner takes home extra."

Garth leaned back in his chair and sipped at his third cup of coffee. There was a lot to learn about this rodeo business, and Dana being so involved was going to make seeing her difficult. But he didn't consider it an insurmountable obstacle. "So when are we going out?" Garth asked over the lip of his cup.

"Going out?" Dana choked on her Coke. She thought she'd explained at his garage why she couldn't go out with him. And after last night...

"And what would you like to do? See a movie? Have dinner? Maybe go to a play?"

"Garth, I can't go out with you. Until that mortgage is taken care of, I can't go out with anyone."

"Your financial problems are an inconvenience, not a reason to stay home."

His fingers were wrapped around his cup. The night before, at The Back Corral, she'd noticed the ring that had been missing from his finger Friday night. It was silver and turquoise—large and very masculine. He was still wearing it, and her eyes focused on the rough-cut stone. It was easier than looking into his penetrating eyes. "Garth, it wouldn't work out between us."

"Dana, how do you know that? You haven't given us a chance."

"I know we live in different worlds."

He pointed at her empty plate. "We both like our eggs over easy, hash browns and whole-wheat toast. We can't be all that different."

"You said it yourself: you're city, I'm country."

"A city boy can drive out to the country sometimes. What night would be best?"

"I work Windrunner every night," she reminded him.

"Doesn't that horse need a break sometime—don't you?"

Once again her eyes met with his. "Garth, if you raced motorcycles, you should understand. Both Windrunner and I have to be in top physical condition. I can't be taking breaks whenever I feel like it. I'm not going out with you."

He blew out a breath, frustrated. He'd chased her and she'd run. He'd asked her out and she'd refused. And refused. And refused. There came a time when a man had to give up. The waitress brought the bill, and he picked it up.

"Garth, let me pay for breakfast," she insisted, putting out her hand for the bill.

"My treat." He stood and got his wallet out of his back pocket.

"But you've done so much already. Fixing my truck for almost nothing, following me home. It's the least I could do."

He shook his head. "Consider it my contribution to saving the family farm."

She grimaced. That did sound corny. "Well, thank you."

At her truck, Dana stopped and reached out to touch Garth's arm. "You're not going to follow me all the way home, are you?"

"Do you want me to?" He already knew her answer.

"No."

"Then I won't." He was through pushing himself on her.

"Thank you." Rising up on her toes, she kissed him. Lightly her lips moved over his. She wanted that feeling—the magic and electricity—just one more time. She wanted the warmth and excitement. But Garth didn't move, didn't touch her, didn't respond to her kiss—and the feeling never came. After a while she gave up and stepped back. Numbly, she stared at him.

"And what was that for?" he asked coldly.

Dana felt hurt and embarrassed. "Nothing, I guess." Turning away, she started for the truck, then paused and looked back. "No, that's not true. That kiss was for something. It was for being such a neat guy."

There were tears in her eyes, and that surprised him. "Would you be honest with me if I asked you a question?"

"It depends on the question."

"Do you like me?" He sure didn't know. One minute she was warm and responsive, the next she was pulling away, telling him it just wouldn't work.

She half laughed. "What a question."

"So what's the answer?"

Turning back toward her truck, she jerked open her door. "Yes," she said angrily, not looking at him. "Too damn much."

Watching her climb into the cab, Garth smiled.

5

"HOLD ON to the horn, Billy. I do it all the time," Dana called to the boy bouncing precariously on Windrunner's back.

"You do?" His adolescent voice cracked and the thirteen-year-old reached forward to find the saddle horn.

"Sure, I do. You can't win in barrel racing if you fall off. Now, smile. You're having fun, remember?"

Eyes straight ahead, his chin lifted high, Billy managed a tense smile. Dana knew he wanted, more than anything, to stay in the saddle. For most beginning riders, sitting the trot wasn't easy. For a boy who couldn't see where he was going, it had to be even more difficult.

Behind Billy, smiling broadly, bounced eight-year-old Katie. "I don't need to hold on, Dana. See? I good now. When can we run?"

"Soon. But only for a little while. It's too hot tonight." Dana had learned that Katie would run old HoJo to death if given the opportunity.

"Danny's comin'," cried Katie, waving a hand toward the barn. "Who with him?"

Dana turned to look. Walking slowly from the barn toward the pasture she used as a riding ring was her brother and a darkly tanned, broad-shouldered man wearing a white, ribbed tank top, navy blue shorts and blue-and-white running shoes. *It can't be,* she told herself, but knew it was. Immediately a thousand butterflies took flight in her stomach.

Quickly Dana looked back at her two students. "Walk your horses," she ordered, and watched to make certain both Billy and Katie obeyed her command.

"It's a man," Katie announced, patting HoJo as the old bay gelding slowed to a walk.

"My dad?" asked Billy, looking toward Dana.

"No, not your dad. It's someone I met last weekend. Walk those horses for a while. No cantering until I say so, Katie."

The girl nodded but Dana knew she'd have to keep an eye on her. Katie's memory wasn't very long. Moving from the middle of the ring, Dana walked toward the railing. She reached the weathered white boards at the same time Danny and Garth did.

"He said he knows you," her brother stated skeptically.

Dana's eyes were on Garth's face. Last Sunday, when he'd beeped his horn in farewell and turned off the freeway in Kalamazoo, she'd told herself she didn't want to see him again. She'd also told herself she could easily forget him, wipe him entirely out of her mind. She'd been wrong.

For three days and nights, Garth Roberts had invaded her thoughts and dreams. While driving her truck to and from work, she'd constantly recalled, in complete detail, how they'd met and the time they'd spent together. And at the office, more than once she'd caught herself daydreaming about dusky blue eyes. Nights, however, were the worst; then the memory of Garth's kisses created a longing she wasn't sure how to handle.

He leaned on the fence, close to her, his eyes on her face. "How ya doin'?"

"Fine. I'm surprised to see you."

"Really?" His eyebrows rose.

She grinned. "Maybe not. You seem to have a way of popping up when least expected."

Chuckling, he looked out across the pasture. "I just thought I'd take a drive out and see where you lived."

He wanted to make his presence sound casual. Her smile said she wasn't angry, and outside the restaurant she'd admitted she liked him, but she hadn't sounded happy about it. "How's your truck doing? No more problems with that wheel-bearing, I hope."

"None. The truck's fine. At least as fine as it's gonna be."

"You the guy that fixed her truck?" asked Danny.

"That's me." Garth looked down at the lanky boy by his side. Danny's hair was lighter than his sister's—more sun-streaked—but his eyes were as dark and just as penetrating.

"It still don't sound right."

"Doesn't sound right," corrected Dana.

"I brought some parts with me," Garth said, looking back at her. "If you're going to be around, I'll work on it tonight."

"You're going to give it a tune-up? Here?" She glanced up at her house, across the road from the horse barn. Her truck was parked by her side door.

Garth also looked in the direction of her place. He'd been surprised when he stopped at the main farmhouse to discover Dana lived separately from her family. The small aluminum-sided house, Danny had informed him on the way to find Dana, had once been the hired hand's home; three years ago Dana had moved into it. "If you've got an extension cord, I should be able to do everything that's necessary right where it stands," Garth told her.

"I know where an extension cord is," Danny said.

Over her shoulder, Dana checked on Billy and Katie. They were still walking their horses, but she knew Katie would soon be begging to canter. "I can't help you. These kids have at least another half hour of riding, then we've got to take care of the horses."

Garth studied Dana's two young pupils. The girl, he could tell, was the one Dana had said had Down's syndrome. It took him a bit longer to realize the boy was blind. He could understand why she wouldn't be able to leave them. "No problem."

DANNY TOOK GARTH back to the farmhouse, found the extension cord and rode with him to Dana's place. Even after helping carry Garth's equipment over to the truck, the boy didn't leave, and Garth soon realized he intended to stick around while he worked.

"Dana's tryin' to win a new truck," Danny said, watching Garth lift the hood of the old Ford. "If she does, then she's gonna get ridda this one. She says she's tired of workin' on a bucket of bolts."

"Your sister works on this truck?" Garth asked, looking in at the V-8 engine.

"Yeah. And my dad. I'm learnin', too. Round here, if somethin' goes wrong, we gotta fix it."

Imitating Garth, Danny leaned over the fender and stared at the engine. "Did you know Dana's a barrel-racing champ? She's gonna win a lot of money. Mom says she hopes so, otherwise we're gonna have to move. I don't wanna move. Do you like cows?"

Garth stepped back from the truck and squatted down to open his toolbox. "I don't know. I guess so."

"Well, I like 'em. I've got twenty calves this year. When I grow up and this farm is mine, I'll have hundreds."

Garth now could understand the pressure Dana had on her. If the farm went, so would Danny's youthful dreams.

"You know, you're the first guy that's been out to see Dana since she moved back. You gonna be her boyfriend?"

That was a question he wasn't sure how to answer. "Let's say, your sister interests me."

Danny grunted. "Dana's always sayin' nobody interests her, and she don't—doesn't wanna get married. Mom says it's 'cause she got hurt once."

He was learning a lot about Dana Allen through her brother. It wasn't his nature to pry, but he couldn't be blamed if the boy talked a lot. "Want to help?"

"Sure." Eagerly, Danny came over to the toolbox.

IT WAS AFTER eight o'clock before Billy's dad and Katie's mother picked them up. The two children had finished their lesson, sponged down the horses and put them out to pasture. Then Katie helped Dana muck out stalls, and Billy rubbed saddle soap into the tack. Now they were gone, and it was time for Dana to face Garth.

Walking from the barn to her house, she had to smile. At the moment, facing either Garth or Danny would take some doing. From beneath the hood of her Ford projected two rear ends, one slender, covered with ragged cutoffs and joined to a pair of long, skinny legs. It was the other posterior that held her attention. She could understand why some men pinched women's bottoms. The idea of walking up and giving Garth's hindquarters a pinch or a pat was very tempting. What she'd give for hips that narrow and cheeks that firm. Of course, he could keep the hair-covered thighs.

"How's it going?" she asked as she neared her truck.

Abruptly two heads came up and out from under the hood. Man and boy turned together to face her. "Man, he's got *everything* pulled apart!" Danny exclaimed.

That didn't sound reassuring. "The question is, can he put everything back together?"

Her eyes met with Garth's. She sure hoped so. She needed that truck to get to work in the morning, and from Friday through Sunday she had rodeos in Illinois, Indiana and Ohio.

"Don't you trust me?" Garth, his eyebrows raised and a grin curving his lips, cocked his head slightly.

"Does a chicken trust a fox?"

His smile widened. "Don't be chicken."

She was chicken about some things, and getting involved with this man was one of them. She was drawn to him, yet afraid. He made her feel good, but she knew he could also hurt her.

From the main farmhouse came a woman's sharp call. "Daniel James!"

Danny scowled. "Oh-oh, I forgot to clean the back porch. Mom always gets all upset about that. Gotta go, Garth. Can you finish without me?"

"No problem, partner. Thanks for your help."

Garth and Dana watched Danny lope down the slope of her lawn, across the gravel road, then up the hill toward the larger farmhouse. When the boy was halfway home, Dana looked back at Garth. "How long will it take you?"

He glanced over his shoulder at the engine. "A half hour, give or take a little."

She had to laugh. "Well, let's not give too much. I do need to get to work in the morning."

"Oh, you'll make it. How often do you work with those kids?"

"Every Wednesday night. Katie's been coming for quite a while, but Billy just started. I have another student, too. Cindy. She's really getting good. When Cindy's on a horse, you can hardly tell she has a problem. She's on vacation this week."

Garth turned back to his work. "How do you handle three students with just two horses?" He remembered she'd said she needed more.

"I also use Danny's pinto, Charlie. He was in the barn when you were down there." Dana didn't get too close to Garth. With his rump back up in the air, she didn't trust herself. The man's hind side was simply too enticing for his own good.

Besides, she could see just fine from where she stood. He was deftly replacing the parts lying on the fender. And, from her own experience under the hood, she could tell he knew exactly what he was doing. That was reassuring.

"So, how's life been treating you?" he asked, stretching across the engine to check a wire.

"Fine." She found her eyes locked on sinewy thighs. Were those muscles as hard as they looked? And how would the hairs feel against her skin?

Shocked by her thoughts, Dana stepped farther back. She needed to get away from this man, needed to stop thinking about his body. "If you're going to be a while, I think I'll put a load of clothes in to wash."

"I'll be a while." He'd hoped she'd stay and talk to him.

Looking toward the setting sun, she wiped her arm across her forehead. It was still a sticky, hot night. "Would you like to go swimming later?"

He poked his head out from under the hood, unsure if he'd heard right. "Swimming?"

"We've got a pond."

"I don't have a suit with me."

"You don't need one." She often jumped into the water with her clothes on. That was one advantage of a pond over a pool. Pools needed to be treated with chemicals and kept clean. Ponds? Well, ponds were ponds.

"Sounds great, then." He certainly hadn't expected her to invite him to go skinny-dipping. Now he was glad he'd taken the chance and driven out.

"Get that engine back together and we'll go."

Dana went inside and threw a load of clothes into the washer, took a quick sponge bath, put on her bikini, then pulled her T-shirt and jeans back on. In half an hour, she was back outside.

"That should do it," Garth proclaimed, tossing a wrench into his toolbox as she neared the truck. He wiped his hands on a rag, then dropped the hood. "Get in and start it up. Let's see how it sounds to you."

Dana did. Having spent hours on the road with the old Ford, she knew its sound, but what she heard when she turned the key this time was different. "What did you do to it?" she asked, leaning out the window. A steady purr now came from the engine.

"A bit of Roberts magic." He grinned, pleased with her response.

"I guess it *is* magic. I've sure never been able to get it to sound this good." She turned off the motor, slid out of the truck and started for the house. "I'll get my checkbook and pay you."

"Forget the checkbook, this one's on me. I wanted to be sure we'd get from one rodeo to the next."

"We?" The word stopped her midstep.

"I thought maybe you'd like a buddy this weekend, someone to help with the driving."

Dana said nothing, but turned slowly to face him. The man interested her, but a weekend of driving, eating and *sleeping* together? She wasn't ready for that. Not yet.

He could sense a refusal coming and hurried to list the reasons he'd thought of why he should go. "Look at it this way: if I come along, you'll be more refreshed and better able to compete in each of the rodeos. You'll do better and win more money."

Winning more money sounded good, but she wondered about being more refreshed.

"You don't have anyone you're going with, do you?"

"No."

"And you could use a driving partner, couldn't you?"

The truth was, she could. It was the other aspect of the partnership that worried her. "And just where do you plan on sleeping? In the cab again?"

"If that's where you want me." He certainly hoped not. It had taken two days before he'd worked the kinks out of his back from his last night there. "I'd rather hoped we might share that mattress of yours in the back or get a motel room."

That was what she'd been afraid of. "No. No sharing my mattress and no motel rooms."

His eyebrows rose. "I thought you said you liked me."

"Like," she repeated. "I didn't say I was ready to hop into bed with you."

He wished he could read her mind. She had him confused. Totally confused. Her kisses promised far more than her words did. Damn, even her words had him baffled. She'd go swimming in the buff with him, but she wouldn't sleep with him. She liked him, but she didn't *like* liking him. Well, he had two choices: play the game her way or forget her. The problem was, the past few days had proven the latter choice impossible.

"Okay, we sleep separate...at least, as long as you want it that way. I've got a sleeping bag I could bring along. It wouldn't be the first time I've slept under the stars."

His agreeing to her terms surprised her. "You're sure?"

"If that's the way you want it." He hoped she'd change her mind. Sleeping under the stars was all right, but he'd much prefer sleeping with her.

"Scout's honor?" She held up her right hand.

He also held up his. "I wasn't a Boy Scout, but I consider myself a man of honor."

Dana had a feeling he was. Actually, his idea of their spending three days together was a good one. She'd bet by Sunday night he'd be ready to admit they were totally different. And she could use a driving buddy.

She still hadn't said yes and that worried Garth. "So, what do you think?"

"I think maybe you're crazy."

"Maybe." He wouldn't disagree. A man in his right mind certainly wouldn't ignore his work when he should be making some major decisions. And a man in his right mind wouldn't keep going after a woman who insisted she had no time for him. But he was. "So?"

"So, let me think about it for a while, okay? Meanwhile, let's go swimming."

He had a feeling she was going to see how things worked out between them tonight and base her decision on that. Well, he hoped things worked out very well. "Ready any time you are."

"Good. I want to see how this baby really runs. Climb on in," she said, sliding back behind the steering wheel.

Garth obediently climbed into the passenger side, pulling the door closed at the same time Dana put the truck into gear. He braced himself against the dash as she bounced out her driveway onto the gravel road. A hundred yards farther, she turned onto another dirt drive that ran on past acres and acres of head-high corn.

Bouncing over ruts and mounds, the truck headed for a dense stand of trees.

"The engine sounds great," she said. A quick turn to the right took them directly toward an oval-shaped pond. Along the neatly mowed grassy bank, she stopped.

"Nice," he admired, glancing around. *And secluded.* The surrounding trees and corn offered plenty of privacy. The short, cropped grass would make a nice bed. He knew from experience what swimming nude with a woman usually led to. By Friday night she shouldn't object to sharing her mattress. He opened his door and stepped out. Dana slid out the other side.

Looking over the hood of the truck, he saw her pull her shirt over her head. Immediately he pulled off his shirt. He'd just started to push down his shorts, when she walked past. "Last one in's a turkey," she challenged.

Abruptly he stopped undressing.

She was wearing a bathing suit. Not that it covered a lot of her, but it did cover the strategic points. And that bothered him. It wasn't that he was modest, but to him skinny-dipping meant both parties went without clothes.

At the edge of the pond, Dana turned and looked back. She'd expected him to be by her side by now, or at least right behind her. Seeing him standing next to the truck, his fingers looped into his waistband, his shorts pushed down on his hips, she wasn't sure what was up. "Aren't you coming in?"

"You've got a suit on."

Dana frowned. Of course she did. "And you've got your shorts."

He looked down, then quickly hiked his shorts back up. "Right."

Once again he'd gotten his signals crossed. Laughing, Garth emptied his pockets on the hood of the truck, then took off his tennis shoes. Someday he'd figure this woman out, but it might not be tonight.

Dana decided not to wait for him, and entered the pond. Although the sun was low on the horizon, the air was still stifling hot and the cold water felt refreshing. Swimming out to the center, she rolled over onto her back and gazed up at the pink-tinged clouds moving slowly across the pale blue sky.

Several minutes passed before she realized Garth still hadn't joined her. Looking toward the bank, she saw him standing at the edge, staring intently at the water. Lazily she swam closer to shore, stopping when she knew she could touch bottom. "Come on in, it's great," she called.

"I can't see the bottom out where you are," he said, his brow slightly furrowed.

"It's here. It goes out gradually for about five feet, then drops off. You can swim, can't you?"

"Sure, I can swim." He tentatively tested the water with a toe. Immediately he pulled his foot back. "It's cold."

She laughed at his shocked expression. "Of course, it's cold. It's spring fed."

Gritting his teeth, he boldly stepped forward. If she could endure the freezing temperature, so could he. His foot touched the icy water, then the sole of his foot reached the bottom—or what he expected to be the bottom. Instead, a soft, slimy muck encompassed his foot. Again he jerked his leg back.

Dana saw his reaction and couldn't restrain her laughter. "It's not going to eat you. Haven't you ever swum in a pond before?"

"No," he admitted, wondering how a man kept up a macho image when all his instincts were telling him to stay out of the water.

Grinning, Dana stood and moved toward him, hands outstretched. "Come on, Mr. Roberts, don't be afraid. Nothing's going to eat you. We haven't lost a visitor in months."

"Thanks," he grumbled, annoyed that she was getting so much entertainment at his expense, and that she looked so damned cool and refreshed. He was roasting.

Reaching the bank, Dana took his hands. "Come on, Garth. It's just like swimming in a swimming pool." She took a step backward, into the water.

"Swimming pools have solid bottoms, not slime—and you can see the bottom," he complained, but he followed her lead.

"It's a little mucky right there, but the bottom gets better as soon as you're away from the edge," she assured him, going back farther.

"What's that?" He pulled his leg up as something under the water slid across his ankles.

"There's a patch of weeds right here. Don't worry about them." She kicked with her foot, trying to uproot any others in their path. "We try to keep them down, but it's almost impossible to get rid of all of them. They won't hurt you."

His trepidation amused her. She'd swum in this pond since she was a child. To her the water promised adventure and pleasure. It was certainly nothing to fear. "Come on, admit it, doesn't that feel nice?"

He was up to his hips and did feel cooler. Also the bottom, away from the edge, was firmer. Perhaps he was being a chicken. He stopped letting her drag him in and took a long step forward, closing the gap between them. He was through being the wimp. It was time he started acting like a man.

"Hi," he murmured seductively, drawing her close. Then he gasped. Her cold, wet bikini top against his warm dry chest was a shock. Immediately he pulled back.

"Hi," she said, laughing. "Cooling off?"

"Definitely." The initial shock over, he wrapped his arms around her back and brought her close again. On the outside he was cooler; inside, his blood was boiling. Ever since he'd seen her tonight, standing in the middle of that pasture, he'd wanted to kiss her.

"Garth—" she wiggled to free herself from his grasp "—we're here to swim. Remember?"

"We'll swim." However, he wasn't ruling out the possibility of their participating in other activities. The more she wiggled, the more her body rubbed against his.

When her hips touched his, she could feel the effect she was having on him. Immediately she stopped moving.

"Did you miss me?" he asked huskily.

He was gazing down at her face, and the warmth in his eyes was enticing, the nearness of his body disconcerting. She liked knowing she could arouse him, but she wasn't going to tell him that, or that she'd missed him. No way. With a teasing grin, she cocked her head to the side. "Why would I miss you?"

He smiled and brushed his lips over the tip of her nose. "Because I missed you. Did I ever tell you how cute you are?"

"Puppies are cute," Dana corrected, pretending to pout.

"Puppies . . . and cowgirls with bangs that hang over their eyes when they're wet—" with one finger he pushed the wet locks aside so he could see her eyes better "—and dark brown eyes that promise ecstasy."

She wasn't sure what her eyes were promising, but his smoldering gaze heated her from head to toe. His fingertip moved from her forehead to her cheek, and a sizzling fire streaked through her body until she almost expected the water around her to start boiling. "Garth, I think—"

"You think too much," he interrupted. Tipping her head back, he covered her mouth with his.

His kiss was a welcome relief. For three nights, memories of the feel of his lips on hers, of the strength of his arms and the gentleness of his touch had left her restless and wanting. For three nights she'd wondered if she'd imagined his kisses were different from all others she'd shared.

Now those memories were reality, and she knew her imagination hadn't been working overtime. Wonderful feelings wrapped around her, blocking out all concerns. Ripples of excitement spread and grew. Lips pressed together in passion said more than words. There was only one thing she wanted: to be held and kissed, just like this.

Above their heads birds sang in the trees; behind them frogs croaked and not far away a truck engine whined. Suddenly Dana stiffened in Garth's grasp. "Oh, no," she groaned.

"Oh, yes," he soothed, kissing several spots on her face in rapid succession.

Breathlessly she tried to explain. "Garth, we've got to stop."

"Not yet, Dana. Not yet." His arms held her possessively close, his need a hard reality.

She knew there wasn't much time. And she knew he wasn't listening. Abruptly she twisted her body, putting them both off balance. Kicking her feet, she used the water as an ally. Together they toppled, both going under.

Garth let go as soon as the water covered his head. He came up sputtering, choking and angry. She was a tease. A blatant tease. "Dammit, Dana Allen, not again!"

She made certain there was some distance between them. The blue of his eyes was dark with anger, his jaw rigid. In a half whisper, she tried to make him understand. "My family, they're here."

Garth jerked his head around to see over his shoulder. Another truck had pulled up next to Dana's, an even older Ford that showed years of hard use. Out of the bed jumped Danny, and from the cab came Dana's parents.

Looking back at Dana, he took in a deep breath, then issued a low warning. "Someday."

Her eyebrows rose and she whispered back. "Someday?"

He didn't say anything for a minute, forcing his body to relax, then murmured, "Someday we won't stop."

With a smile, he turned and faced her family.

He'd met her mother when he first stopped at the farmhouse. The short, dark-haired woman was slightly overweight and in her late forties. There was some resemblance between mother and daughter, but seeing Dana's father for the first time, Garth decided Dana looked more like him. She'd definitely inherited the balding man's lean build and dark brown eyes.

"Hi," Dana called to them. "Water's great." She should have known they'd show up. With her house visible from the farmhouse, the entire family had undoubtedly known exactly when she and Garth left her place and where they'd gone. In a way it was surprising they'd waited this long to come.

Garth wondered what position her family might have found them in if they'd arrived ten minutes later. It could have been embarrassing.

Her father stooped down and swished the water with his hand. "Water's warm."

"Warm?" repeated Garth, finding the description far from accurate.

"Warmer than it was last month," Dana informed him. "Mom, Dad, this is Garth Roberts, the man who fixed my truck last Friday."

"We met at the house," her mother explained.

Her father nodded. "Danny said you've been working on my daughter's truck tonight."

"And he's got it purrin' like a kitten, Dad," Dana responded.

Garth could feel the older man's eyes boring into him, scrutinizing and judging. It had been a long time since he'd had to pass a father's inspection. The women he'd dated in the past five years had been on their own, and whether his intentions were honorable or not had never been the question. In fact he'd sometimes wondered what *their* intentions were.

Finally her father stood and began to take off his boots. "Glad you came out. That old truck's needed a tune-up for ages."

Dana's mother kicked off a pair of thongs and stepped into the water. "Oh, now, that feels good." She sighed and waded in until the water came to just below her knee-length shorts.

As soon as her father's boots were off, he rolled up the cuffs of his denim overalls and also entered the pond. "Ahh." He sighed in satisfaction. "Nothing like a little cool water to make the heat bearable."

Only Danny had on a pair of swimming trunks. He ran in, then made a shallow dive, coming up next to Garth. "You got everything back in?"

"Everything I could find."

"Sometimes Dad ends up with somethin' extra. He usually just tosses it in a box. I can swim across and back. Can you?"

"I don't know." Garth eased himself down so the water covered his shoulders. He swam enough at the Y to know he could handle the distance. It was the territory he didn't like. The opposite side of the pond was definitely weedy.

"You don't know?" Danny looked surprised.

"He isn't used to swimming in a pond. He only swims in pools—nice weed-free pools where he can see the bottom and knows it's safe," Dana explained, grinning.

Looking across the pond, Garth decided the weeds weren't all that bad. At least, he hoped they weren't. "Let's see if I can or can't," he said to Danny.

"Good. A race? Over and back? Last one's a turkey?"

"Now, where have I heard that before?" He grinned at Dana, then looked back at the boy. "Okay, over and back. Last one's a turkey."

Danny made a standing dive, swimming several feet underwater before surfacing. Garth kept his head above the water, watching where he was going.

It wasn't hard for him to keep up with the ten-year-old, and he could easily have passed him, but he didn't. He preferred to let Danny lead the way. Not that Danny took a route that missed the weeds. Garth hated the feel of them touching his fingertips and knew there was no way he was going to put his feet down and have the weeds wrap around his legs.

Before they reached the bank, Danny turned and headed back. Garth lost a little distance but made it up. Still he didn't try to pass Danny. He wouldn't be proving anything by beating a child a third his age, and considering that he'd faced the weeds and survived, he felt like a winner. When he reached Dana's side, he stood up. He was ready to congratulate himself when something moved under his foot.

Dana saw him jump to the side, his jaw rigid, his eyes wide. "What's the matter?"

"Do rocks move?" he asked, knowing they didn't.

She laughed. "No, but turtles do. I suggest you get off his back."

"I did. What kind of turtles?"

"Oh, we have a variety. Box. Snapping."

"Snapping turtles?" He walked out of the pond. At least in a swimming pool, one didn't have to worry about losing a toe.

Dana followed him out.

"When I was a boy," her dad said, "we used to go skinny-dippin' in here. I was always afraid one of those snappers would take off my you-know-what."

Garth flinched at the idea. Maybe it was a good thing Dana had worn a bathing suit and he'd kept on his shorts.

Plopping down on the grass, Dana wondered what Garth thought of her father. Dan Allen certainly looked the hayseed tonight. He hadn't even changed from the dirty overalls he'd worn all day. Not that she cared. Her father was a hardworking farmer, and she loved him.

She'd been embarrassed by him once, when she'd seen him through John's eyes. Looking back, she knew her parents were one reason John had wanted her to move into the city. He'd wanted her to divorce herself from their influence so he could make her over into the kind of woman he wanted. The day they broke up, he'd even admitted he'd hated it every time he'd had to drive out to the farm and spend time with her family.

Thank goodness she'd grown up enough to appreciate her parents for their good points. It didn't matter that they hadn't finished high school and weren't worldly and sophisticated. They were honest, caring people, who willingly gave their time, their love and their money to their children. She owed them for that.

"Can't remember a hotter summer," her mother commented, coming out of the pond. Her father followed. Neither had gone in much above the knees, but both looked refreshed. Danny stayed in, swimming and diving.

"They say we've had record highs of both heat and humidity," responded Garth, sitting down near Dana.

Strolling over to lean against his truck, her father added his opinion. "I remember back thirty years ago...."

While Garth and her parents discussed the weather, Dana combed her fingers through her wet hair. Plaiting the thick locks into a French braid, she listened as the topic turned to the latest news. Then her father mentioned the Tigers, and Dana discovered Dan Allen and Garth Roberts had a mutual interest. Pitchers were named, first basemen and fielders. Each knew players' batting averages, the number of home runs hit that season and debated who had made the most errors.

When her hair was finished, Dana looked at her mother, grinned and shook her head. Her mother laughed. "We've lost them, dear." Pushing herself up off the grass, the older woman headed toward the truck. "I've got a fresh blueberry pie up at the house. Anyone interested in going with me?"

"I am!" yelled Danny, scrambling out of the water.

"Sounds good to me," agreed Dana's father. "Come on, Garth. Mother makes the best blueberry pie in the country."

IT WAS AFTER ELEVEN when they left her parents' house. Crickets sang and clouds covered the sky, blocking out the stars and moon. In the darkness they stood beside Garth's

Bronco, and he took her hand in his. "So, what about this weekend? Have you made up your mind?"

Dana looked down at their entwined hands. His silver and turquoise ring pressed against her fingers, but his hold was gentle. The hold he was taking on her life was just as gentle, but it scared her. "I think you're wasting your time. I don't think it'll work between us."

"We won't know if we don't give it a try, will we?"

"One of us might get hurt."

"That's possible," he agreed. Bringing her knuckles to his lips, he lightly kissed them.

The touch sent shivers down her spine and she blew out a shaky breath. "Garth, we're so different."

"*Vive la différence*," he proclaimed huskily, and pulled her to him.

6

THEY LEFT EARLY Friday morning and didn't start back until after dark Sunday. For those three days, Garth discovered what it was like to haul a horse over hundreds of miles of highway, sleep when and where he could, and eat dust. He also began to learn the names of the cowgirls who competed against Dana and saw over and over again the pressure she was under.

Each rodeo was different. Although the barrels were always placed the same distance apart and in the same pattern, sometimes the turf was hard and fast, sometimes mushy and slow. And the position of the outside railing could confuse a horse. He'd seen them nearly run into the barrier, and that scared him. The more he got to know Dana, the more her safety concerned him.

That she placed in the money two out of the three shows seemed great to Garth, but Dana wasn't happy. She'd taken a fourth at the all-important IPRA rodeo in Angola, while teenage Connie Birch had placed first. "That's the one that counts for the regional championship. We're neck and neck again," Dana explained on the way back to the farm.

Garth watched the road as he drove. "Someone said her parents paid twenty thousand dollars for that horse she rides."

Resting her head against the seat, Dana closed her eyes. "If she wins the regional, they'll have made back their money."

"Why keep doing this, Dana? Between the gas you've used, the wear and tear on your truck, food, Cokes and entry fees, at most you cleared two hundred dollars this weekend. If you need twenty thousand dollars, why not just sell Windrunner and give the money to your father?"

Wearily she turned her head and looked at him. He obviously didn't hold any high hopes for her. "No one wants to pay twenty thousand for Win. I don't know if I can explain it, but a horse that wins for one rider won't necessarily win for another. A special relationship has to be there, where horse and rider work as a team."

"Sort of like the chemistry between a man and a woman, eh? If it's there, wow—if not, you can just forget it." He glanced her way. With Dana the chemistry was definitely there. He'd felt it from their first kiss.

"Sort of, I guess." She chose not to follow up on that idea. It was safer to keep the discussion to money and horses. "I was going to sell Windrunner earlier this year. A few gals tried him, but he just wouldn't go for them, not like he does for me. Five thousand was the most anyone offered. I can make that much on his back."

"You can make it, but you're taking a chance on being hurt or just plain wearing yourself out. How long can you hit every rodeo within five hundred miles and hold down a job?"

"Until the end of October. I have no choice."

"Everyone has choices."

Her eyes narrowed. "Name mine, Garth."

"Borrow the money."

She laughed. "That's what got us into this predicament in the first place. Plus, who's going to lend us twenty thousand dollars? The banks certainly aren't and our friends are in as tight a financial situation as we are. I don't know about you, but I don't know too many people with twenty thousand dollars just lying around." She didn't know *anyone* with that kind of money to loan.

Garth said nothing. If he could have, he would have loaned her the money, but his capital was tied up in the expansion of Roberts's Auto Center.

She faced forward again and wearily muttered her conclusion. "My only choice is to try for the Primo Feed award."

"I guess so," he conceded, but he didn't like it.

They drove on in silence.

GARTH LEFT HER Sunday night with a promise to call. She wondered if he would. Whether he realized it or not, she'd been testing him. She'd turned him into her gofer, made him help with Windrunner—even though she could tell he wasn't at ease around the horse—and had given him no sexual encouragement. He'd slept on the ground in the sleeping bag he'd brought along, while she'd slept on the mattress in the back of the truck. And she hadn't allowed more than a chaste kiss now and then. She'd wanted to see how he'd react.

The problem was he'd reacted just fine, doing as she asked with a smile and accepting her restraints on their relationship with no arguments. The more time she spent with the man, the more she liked him. He was a nice guy— definitely citified, but nice. Something deep inside still warned her not to get involved, but she was finding that warning harder and harder to heed.

When Garth didn't call Monday or Tuesday, she told herself it was all for the best, but she was disappointed. By Wednesday morning, she knew he wouldn't get hold of her even if he tried. Her boss had given her the rest of the week off as part of her vacation time, and before the sun had cleared the horizon, she was on her way to Illinois.

Four days and as many rodeos later she was home again, road tired but satisfied with her wins. Once again she was ahead of Connie, and she had six hundred dollars to give to her father.

"Any calls?" Dana asked, helping her mother set the table for Sunday dinner.

"For you? No. Were you expecting any?"

"No, not really." She'd merely hoped.

"Maybe one from Garth?" her mother probed, smiling.

"Oh, he said he might call, but I really didn't expect him to. I think last weekend showed him I was right. We're too different."

"Different?" Nancy Allen quirked an eyebrow.

"In our tastes. We don't like the same kind of music, Garth thinks living in the city is great and he's never even ridden a horse, nor does he seem to want to. I could go on.... We're just different."

"Differences make life interesting," her mother insisted, adding butter to the potatoes she was mashing.

Dana could almost hear Garth's smooth, sexy voice saying, *Vive la différence.* "That's not what you said about John."

"John." Nancy Allen stopped mashing and made a face. "John *was* different. He was a snob—a fancy-pants son of a you-know-what."

Dana chuckled. Her mother had never liked John.

"I was never so happy as the day you two broke up. If that man had ended up my son-in-law, I—" she looked at her daughter "—I think I would have disowned you. Don't go comparing Garth to John. Garth is different."

"Well, I'm glad you like Garth more than you did John, but one thing the two have in common is promising to call, then not."

"Maybe he's been busy."

"Sure." Dana laughed sarcastically and changed the subject. Forcing thoughts of Garth to the back of her mind, she helped her mother get the meat and potatoes on the table, then called in her father and brother.

After everyone had eaten and the dishes were done, she headed for the barn. What she needed was a ride, a long, hard ride. A half hour later, mounted on Windrunner, she headed down the lane back to the woods.

Kicking her horse into a lope, she allowed her thoughts about Garth to resurface, and the words bottled up inside spilled out. "Damn you, Garth Roberts, why did I ever have to meet you? Why did you have to follow me to St. Charles? Come out here? Buddy up with me? Why did you have to get under my skin?"

Windrunner's hooves pounded against the hard dirt, and she urged him on to a faster speed, making the wind hit her face and sting her eyes. When she finally slowed him and turned back toward the farm, it was the wind she blamed for the tears sliding down her cheeks.

She didn't even bother trying to explain the smile that sprang to her lips the moment she saw the tan Bronco parked in front of the farmhouse. Her heart racing, she headed for the barn. Two minutes later, while she was still untacking Windrunner, Garth also entered the barn.

"Have a nice ride?" he asked, strolling toward her.

"Great." She remembered the tears and surreptitiously wiped at her cheeks with her arm.

"Your dad said you had a good weekend, that you're ahead of that Birch kid again."

"For a while." So Garth had been there long enough to talk to her folks. She hoped her mother hadn't said anything about her being upset over his not calling.

Garth leaned against the stall door and watched her slip the bridle off Windrunner's head. "Wonder why I didn't call?"

Damn! Her mother had said something. With a slap on the horse's rump, she sent the gelding out to the pasture. Not looking at Garth, she turned to pick up the saddle. "All you said was you might."

He pushed himself away from the stall door and reached her saddle and blanket before she did. "Let me." Easily he hoisted the combination over a shoulder as he'd seen the cowboys at the rodeos do. "Actually, I tried calling you several times. You're going to have to get yourself one of those answering machines. In there?" With his free hand he motioned toward the tack room.

"You called?" Blocking his way, she stared at him, her blood pounding in her ears. Those few words meant more than he would ever realize.

"I started calling Monday evening, both your place and your folks', but no one answered."

"We were probably all outside."

"I wanted to tell you I was going to be out of the country for a few days. My mother and stepfather were on a cruise, and he had a heart attack. I had to fly down to Nassau and give Mom a little emotional support and help get them both back to Florida."

Suddenly Dana felt terrible for all the angry thoughts she'd had. Garth had had an emergency to tend to. That he'd even taken the time to try to get hold of her was amazing. "Your stepfather, is he . . . ?"

"He's in a hospital in Orlando, but I think he's going to be all right." Garth stepped around her and carried the saddle and blanket into the tack room. She followed, bridle in hand. The saddle put up, he took the bridle from her and hung it on its peg. When his hands were free, he cupped her face in his palms. "I tried to get hold of you from Nassau, too. I missed you, Dana. I even sent you a letter. I gather you haven't gotten it."

"No." Looking into the blue of his eyes, she could feel herself relaxing. He had gotten under her skin, and at the moment, it was a nice feeling.

"How are you?" he asked softly.

"Fine," she said and meant it. Every second he was with her, she was feeling better.

"You look tired." Gently he ran his thumbs over her cheeks, rubbing away the tearstains, then he lowered his head and kissed her—lightly and tenderly. "You're right, you are fine," he murmured, and slid his arms around her, drawing her close. "Very fine."

His mouth became more demanding, and Dana was glad. Chaste kisses and a platonic relationship no longer sounded good. She'd missed him and was glad to be in his embrace again. Wrapping her arms around his back, she held him tight.

After spending a week thinking of her, wanting her, Garth found it difficult to keep his need under control. When he lifted his head, breathing heavily, he knew he either had to find something else for them to do or he was going to drag her off to bed. "Want to go for a drive?"

"A drive?" she asked shakily.

"Maybe get an ice cream?" He'd seen an ice-cream parlor in the village of Clay.

"Sure." Ice cream wasn't exactly what she wanted, either, but it would be a whole lot safer.

NO SOONER HAD THEY stepped into the air-conditioned ice-cream parlor, when she heard a familiar, quavery voice. "Whaddya know, Dana Allen's out for a bit of frozen cow juice. How's the prettiest gal in Clay doin' tonight? And when you gettin' married?"

Hal Hoffman was a lean, weathered septuagenarian who'd been a farmer all his life and an old family friend for as long as Dana could remember. From her earliest recall, he'd been asking her when she was getting married. Before puberty, she'd always said "Never." Later, like most teenagers, she'd had hopes and dreams. And after most of her schoolmates did marry, she took up teasing him back. "Tomorrow. Didn't you get the invitation I sent?"

"Nope, but I'll be there." He smiled a toothless grin at Garth and held out a wrinkled hand. "You the guy that makes house calls to tune up trucks?"

Garth shook the man's hand, but looked at Dana for an explanation.

"Dad tell you about that, Hal?" she asked.

"Shore did. Said that old truck of yore's is runnin' better than ever." He nodded his approval at Garth. "You ever want to make some more house calls, I got a truck that could use some work. Plus a whole lot of junkers... which they now want me to git rid of." He grunted, disgusted. "City folks. They move out to the country, then wants to make it look like the city, writin' rules about what you kin and cain't have." He waved a finger at Garth. "Let me tell you, there's a lot of farmers around here that's got dozens of old cars and trucks. If they want us to git rid of 'em, they kin come out an git 'em."

"Any old ones? I mean really old ones?" asked Garth. Every car collector dreamed of finding a classic in someone's backyard.

"I've got a 1938 Mack Junior. Ever heard of one of them?"

Garth nodded. He had. Production of the half-ton pickup had been abandoned after 1938 as Mack Trucks concentrated on their heavy-duty trucks. He wasn't sure how many were around, but he knew not many had been made or sold. "What kind of shape is it in?" He suspected the body would be badly rusted out. It was out West, away from the corrosive salt they used on the roads, where the best car and truck finds were made.

"Not bad. That one I've kept in the barn."

Now Garth was even more interested. "Sometime I'd like to see it."

"Stop by any time you like." Hal Hoffman took the cone the girl behind the counter handed him and paid her. After licking the ice cream that was already starting to dribble down the side, he gave Dana a wink and a grin. "What time you say that weddin' was?"

"When I get around to it," she kidded back.

"Better make it soon. I ain't gettin' any younger. See ya 'round," he said to both of them and shuffled out of the shop.

Turning back to the counter, Garth and Dana gave their orders. Their choices were different. He loved chocolate; she hated it. "To each his own," Dana philosophized, refusing to let it bother her.

As soon as they had their ice creams, they walked across the street to the village park and sat down on the one and only bench. "So the wedding's tomorrow?" Garth cocked his head to the side, one eyebrow raised. "Anyone I know?"

Dana concentrated on her cone. "Hal and I have had that routine for years now. If I ever did get married, he'd probably have a heart attack. Speaking of heart attacks, had your stepfather ever had one before?" She wanted to change the subject.

Garth willingly let her. He certainly wasn't ready to discuss marriage. He still wasn't quite sure what it was that

NO COST! NO OBLIGATION!
NO PURCHASE NECESSARY!

PLAY "LUCKY 7"
AND GET AS MANY AS SIX FREE GIFTS . . .

HOW TO PLAY:

1. With a coin, carefully scratch off the three silver boxes at the right. This makes you eligible to receive one or more free books, and possibly other gifts, depending on what is revealed beneath the scratch-off area.

2. You'll receive brand-new Harlequin Temptation® novels, never before published. When you return this card, we'll send you the books and gifts you qualify for absolutely free!

3. And, a month later, we'll send you 4 additional novels to read and enjoy. If you decide to keep them, you'll pay only $2.24 per book, a savings of 26¢ per book. There is no extra charge for postage and handling. There are no hidden extras.

4. We'll also send you additional free gifts from time to time, as well as our newsletter.

5. You must be completely satisfied, or you may return a shipment of books and cancel at any time.

FREE—digital watch and matching pen

You'll love your new LCD quartz digital watch with its genuine leather strap. And the slim matching pen is perfect for writing that special person. Both are yours FREE as our gift of love.

DETACH AND MAIL CARD TODAY

DETACH AND MAIL CARD TODAY

BUSINESS REPLY CARD

First Class   Permit No. 717   Buffalo, NY

Postage will be paid by addressee

Harlequin Reader Service®
901 Fuhrmann Blvd.,
P.O. Box 1867
Buffalo, NY 14240-9952

NO POSTAGE
NECESSARY
IF MAILED
IN THE
UNITED STATES

attracted him to this cowgirl. "No, Ben's always been very healthy. Mom said they never suspected he had a blockage. When she called and told me what had happened, I was worried about how she'd cope. After spending almost a week with her, I left impressed. She's one strong lady." He watched a young mother follow a toddler to the park swings. "But then, I guess after what she went through with my father, she learned to be strong."

"Your father died?"

"No." Garth looked back at Dana. "It might have been easier if he had. My father ran out on us when I was five."

"Divorced your mother?" Nowadays it was certainly a common occurrence.

"A divorce would have been the mature way to face the problem. My father chose to split. One day he was there, the next he wasn't. When Mom finally accepted the fact that he wasn't coming back, she divorced him."

"That must have been hard on you—both of you."

She didn't know how hard, Garth thought. He slipped his arm around Dana's shoulders. He didn't usually talk about his childhood, but he felt like telling her. "It made me angry. Angry with my father for leaving, with my mother for whatever she'd done to make him go, and with the world in general. I was a hellion as a kid, always getting into trouble. One school counselor told my mother I had a lot of hostility pent up inside." He chuckled. "That was after I'd taken a swing at him."

Her heart went out to the deserted child. But Garth didn't seem angry now. "Do you still have a lot of hostility pent up inside?"

"No." He licked at his cone, thinking back. It had taken time. A long time. "Anger is a very destructive emotion. While I was in the hospital, I realized that going around with a chip on my shoulder wasn't going to change things, that my father had been a bastard but I didn't have to turn out that way."

"Your fighting put you in the hospital?" She'd seen men fight—sometimes the cowboys did, especially if they'd been drinking—and she hated it.

"No. A concrete wall put me there," he explained. "Remember I told you I used to race motorcycles?" She nodded. "Well, one day I misjudged a turn—and my speed. The truth is, I was pushing too hard, trying too hard to win." He fixed her with a penetrating stare. "Like you're doing."

Dana looked away. "I'm not pushing too hard." They'd been over this before. "How bad were you hurt?"

"Bad. Just about every inch of me was in some sort of a cast. I had more screws in my body than that Bronco has." He waved his cone toward his car. "The doctors told me it was a miracle I was still alive."

She looked at his car, then at Garth. The thought of him being dead, of their never having met, turned her blood cold. "You're all right now?"

"I thought so, but there's this cowgirl who keeps telling me I've got a screw loose." He grinned and leaned close to rub the tip of his tongue over her lips. "Hmm, not bad, but you really should try chocolate."

The feel of his tongue on her mouth was electrifying; her lips suddenly seemed oversensitized. "I don't like chocolate, I like vanilla," she said shakily, really not caring what flavor she had. What she wanted was for him to kiss her. Instead he sat back, smiled and licked his cone.

When they were finished and walking back to his car, she realized he'd never really answered her question. "Do you ever have any problems as a result of that accident?"

"No problems. It took a while before my back stopped hurting, but now all the bones I shattered have mended and the muscles I tore have been built back up. Doctors say I'm good for at least a hundred thousand miles."

Stopping at the car door, she turned to face him and reached out and touched his arm, letting her fingers glide slowly over a well-developed biceps. He certainly looked and felt fit. Glancing up, she found him watching her, and she smiled. "Just checking the chassis."

"Want to check it out more thoroughly?" he asked, leaning close and grinning provocatively. "I'm afraid it does have a few scars."

"Oh yeah?" She'd seen him in shorts without a shirt on and had noticed one scar on his back. But he'd said "a few." There had to be others, located in an area he'd so far kept covered. Boldly she kept her eyes locked with his. "Maybe some time you'll show me."

"Hey, hey. At last, I'm getting somewhere." He gave her a quick kiss, then stood back and opened the car door for her. He was willing to show her his scars right then, along with a few other features of his body, but the middle of town didn't seem to be the best place.

Driving back to the farm, Dana thought about what Garth had said about his father. "I can't imagine a father walking out on a wife and small child," she said, not even realizing she'd spoken aloud.

Garth glanced her way. Having met her family, he could understand why. He'd been impressed by the closeness of the four Allens, and a little jealous. "Actually, it's not an unusual occurrence." He'd read a lot on the matter. It had helped him to know there were other men like his father; people who simply couldn't cope with the responsibilities of family life. What he'd learned over the years was that it wasn't his fault—or his mother's.

"And you never saw him again?"

"Oh, but I did. It was weird. While I was growing up, I was always dreaming about his coming back or my meeting him someplace. By the time I was twenty-five, I'd given up on the idea of ever seeing him again and didn't think I cared. Then one night, I ran into him at a party."

"You knew who he was?" She wondered if he looked like his father, and if he'd be like his father, shirking responsibilities. Perhaps that was why he'd never married.

"Not right away. It was only after the hostess mentioned that we both had the same last name and similar features that I gave him a closer look. When I went over and talked to him, he was as surprised to find out who I was as I was to find out he was my father."

"Did he tell you why he left?"

"He said he'd never wanted to get married and never wanted a kid and that I should be glad he'd stuck around for five years."

"Sounds like a real compassionate guy."

"He was a gem." That was the last time he'd been in a fight. A lot of years of bitterness had been wiped away with that one punch. "It wasn't what you'd call a joyous reunion."

No, she didn't imagine it had been. "Did you tell your mother?"

"Yes. She said it sounded like him. She was sorry for me, but it didn't bother her. I'm so glad she met and married Ben."

"They live in Kalamazoo?" She wondered if Garth had told his mother about her. Or if she would ever meet the woman. Not that she necessarily wanted to. Her meetings with John's mother had been anything but pleasant. Although her parents had never liked John, they'd been courteous enough not to say anything in front of him. John's mother had openly stated that she didn't think a girl raised on a farm was right for her son—a point of view John later adopted.

"It got so winters were too cold up here for Mom. She and Ben moved down to Orlando ten years ago. When Ben's better, they may come up for a visit. I'll have to introduce you. You and Mom would get along great." He chuckled. "She hates chocolate, too."

"Good for her." Dana already liked the woman. In a world of chocolate lovers, she'd found an ally.

Pulling into her drive, he parked next to her truck and turned in his seat to face her. "What about lunch tomorrow?"

"What *about* lunch tomorrow?" Dana grinned, knowing perfectly well he was asking her out—and that she would go.

"How long do you have? Can you get away? And where would you like to go?"

She laughed. "So many questions."

Leaning over, Garth touched his lips to hers, then murmured, "I don't hear any answers."

"I have an hour. Yes, I can get away. And anywhere you'd like to go would be fine." She wrapped her arms around his neck and kissed him back.

GARTH TOOK HER out to lunch Monday, Tuesday and Wednesday. His letter from Nassau also arrived on Wednesday. When he came out and helped her with the handicapped riders, she showed it to him, and they laughed about the "speed" of the postal system.

She couldn't take Thursday off—she had the payroll to do—but as soon as she got home she loaded up Windrunner. Garth pulled into the drive just as she was about to pull out, jumped into the truck and asked what she was waiting for. Driving as fast as she dared, they arrived at the Mason County Fair just in time to pay her fees and warm up for the barrel-racing event. On the way home, Garth bought her a Coke and a hamburger to celebrate her second-place win.

Friday she left work early and found Garth already at the farm, ready to hitch up the trailer. By eight o'clock she was in Saline, just south of Ann Arbor, waving to the crowd as she loped Windrunner around the arena for the grand entry.

Three hours later, after the rodeo, they were headed back to the farm. They wouldn't know until Sunday how she'd placed, but she'd had a good time and was presently in the lead. "Now for two days of rest, right?" Garth knew she was tired. He was tired. Trying to work full time and go to these rodeos was exhausting. She'd said she'd be staying home that weekend, and he was glad.

"I wish," Dana said, dreading the next two days.

"What do you mean, you wish? I was hoping you'd come into town tomorrow, let me show you my apartment, have dinner with me." He glanced her way. "Get to know each other a little better."

The warm invitation in his eyes suggested they'd get to know each other intimately. And she wanted to. Any reservations she'd had were gone. Why he was sticking around, she wasn't sure, but this had definitely progressed beyond a one-night stand. Only she couldn't see him tomorrow. "I have to help with the hay tomorrow."

"Hay?" He frowned. It wasn't the answer he'd wanted. "How do you help with hay?"

She was continually amazed at how little he knew about farm life. "I have to help put it in the barn."

"All day?" He could see his plans going out the window.

"Probably until the sun sets. Dad wants to get it up before we have any rain. Moldy hay isn't much good for anything but mulch."

"Any chance you could get away early—maybe around two or three o'clock?"

If her dad had found more boys to help, she would have said yes, but this was the weekend of the county fair and all but two able-bodied teenagers were either showing or attending. Even her brother had his calves there and would be out at the fairgrounds all day. Tomorrow her mother would fix dinner, then go to the fair to be with Danny. Dana knew she had no choice; she had to stay and help. "I can't, Garth. Dad needs me."

"And what about me?" He hated feeling jealous of a farm, but it was getting that way.

"Garth, I told you when we met, I—"

"I know," he cut in, glaring into the night. "You don't have time for me."

"It's not that. I mean, I wish I could spend the day with you. It's just—" She wasn't sure what to say. "There's just things I have to do right now. Things I can't get out of. I even had to give up going to two rodeos this weekend to help Dad."

"In other words, in your list of priorities I'm at the bottom."

"No," she protested. He'd become very important to her. Perhaps too important.

"No? Then spend tomorrow with me."

"Don't you understand? I can't. Not tomorrow. Maybe another time."

"Sure." He knew there'd always be something else. The problem was, he did understand. She didn't have time for him—*really* didn't—and that irritated him.

They drove the rest of the way home in silence, but her mind wasn't silent. His anger made her angry. She'd told him how it would be. It wasn't as though this was the way she wanted things to be. She just didn't know what else to do.

Garth left without kissing her. He simply said goodnight and drove off. She'd realized he was upset, but thought he might mention calling her or say he was coming out the next day—or even offer to help with the hay. But he'd said nothing. Watching the taillights of the Bronco disappear over the hill, for the first time ever, Dana hated living on a farm.

In the morning she knew she was going to hate it even more before the day was over. Haying was a hard, dirty job under the best of conditions. With the temperature in the nineties and the humidity as high, putting up hundreds of bales of hay was going to be absolutely miserable.

They started as soon as the dew was gone from the fields: her father, herself and two teenage neighbor boys. Her father drove the tractor that pulled the baler and hay wagon. Automatically the hay was gathered from the windrows where it had been raked to dry. The baler shaped it into solid rectangles and bound them with twine. One by one the bales were catapulted onto the wagon until it was too full to take any more. Then the real work began.

Her father unloaded the bales from the wagon and placed them on a conveyor run by a pulley connected to the tractor. Standing high above the ground at the opening to the loft, with gloved hands Dana pulled each bale off the conveyor and carried it in to the teenage boys. They were the ones who had the back-straining job of lifting and stacking.

Every hour it got hotter and every break it got harder for her to talk herself into going back to work. By mid-afternoon she was beat. Her throat was dry and her skin was damp from the heat and itchy from the irritation of the hay. Her shoulders and back ached, her legs were cramped and she feared her fingers would be permanently clenched in a clawlike position. Lifting another bale from the top of the elevator, she grunted, hunched forward to balance its weight, and carried it forward to the nearest boy. Heading back to the elevator, eyes half closed to avoid the dust and bits of hay in the air, she wondered how much longer she could keep going.

Head down, shoulders stooped, Dana walked straight into a solid, unmoving body. Long, strong fingers wrapped around her arms and a commanding voice said, "Time for you to take a break."

She recognized the turquoise ring and the voice. Eyes opening wide, she looked up. "Garth!"

"Sit!" he ordered, pushing her down on a broken bale near the opening of the loft.

"I can't sit," she insisted, immediately standing back up.

His brow furrowed and his blue eyes clouded. Again he pushed her down. "Sit, I said. Whether you're willing to admit it or not, you're beat."

"So's everyone." She stood again, irritated. "Now, if you'll get out of my way, I have to get these bales to the boys."

Garth glanced toward the back of the loft, where the two teenage boys lounged against the hay, as ready for a break as she was. Their grins said they were enjoying the show. "You—" Garth pointed a finger at one "—she's taking a break. Take over her job."

The boys looked at each other, shrugged, and one started down.

"No!" Dana ordered, stopping him. Then she glared at Garth. "Look, we're shorthanded as it is. They need to stack. I can get the bales to them."

"No, you can't." He pushed her back down to a sitting position. "*I* can." He turned and lifted the bale she'd been after, plus another.

Dana stared at him, dumbfounded. He might think he could help, but he wouldn't last long, not dressed in a tank top and shorts and wearing no gloves. In minutes that hay would be irritating his skin, and it wouldn't take many bales before the twine began cutting into his fingers. "You can't do it," she informed him.

Without looking at her, he carried the bales over to the boys. "Correct that. I *am* doing it."

"You're not going to last long."

He eyed her on his way back for more. "Meaning you're in better shape than I am?"

"Meaning I'm dressed for the job; you aren't."

He did notice that the two boys in the loft had jeans on and were wearing gloves. And looking down at the wagon, he saw her father was wearing overalls and gloves. He decided she might have a point. His legs were already beginning to itch where the first two bales had rubbed. "Then take me up to the house and let me borrow a pair of your dad's overalls."

"What about your back?"

"What about it?" He walked over to the edge of the loft and looked down. Dan Allen was still tossing bales on the conveyor. Waving his arms, Garth got his attention.

"You broke it, didn't you?"

"We're taking a break," he yelled down to the older man, then faced Dana. "You broke your ankle last year. I don't see you sitting around."

"That's different," she argued. The boys, she noticed, were already scooting down from the top of the bales. She knew where they'd be heading—straight for the cooler.

"All right." She gave in, moving toward the ladder. "Let's see if I can find you something to wear."

Her father's overalls looked strange on Garth, and Dana had to force herself not to laugh. On the porch, where they always kept extra gloves—not necessarily matching ones—she found him a pair to protect his hands. Fifteen minutes later they were back up in the loft, and the stack of bales was growing higher.

By the time Dan Allen called it quits for the night, Garth was sure he'd lifted and carried at least a million tons of hay. With a groan, he sank down on the nearest bale and pulled off his gloves. His fingers felt numb and his sweaty skin itched. He'd worked at some pretty grueling jobs in his past, but this one was as hard as any he'd known.

Dana sat next to him and patted the knee of his overalls. "Now, wasn't that fun?"

He groaned again, sending her a sidelong look that said exactly how much fun he'd had.

"Want to go for a swim in the pond?"

"No," he said firmly. It would take a lot more than heat and hay to get him into that pond again.

"How 'bout a shower at my place?"

Turning his head, he looked at her. That suggestion sounded good. "Will you wash my back?"

"I don't know about washing your back, but I will give you a rubdown afterward." He deserved it. His help had allowed them to finish before dark. Whereas she could carry just one bale, Garth easily managed two. And he'd seen to it that all of them took frequent breaks. She'd protested, but her father had gone along with the idea, and in the long run Garth had been right; they had felt fresher and accomplished more.

"It's a deal."

"YOU GO FIRST," Dana said as they entered her place. "I'll make us some sandwiches."

Garth caught her hand before she moved into the kitchen, his grip gentle but firm. Stopping her, he drew her back, turning her so she faced him. "Why don't we take a shower together?"

The question set her heart hammering against her ribs. They were about to move from friends to lovers; they both knew it. Yet Dana didn't feel quite ready to jump into a shower with him. "No, you go first," she repeated, moving back away from him and hoping she sounded more casual than she felt. "Bathroom's the first door to the right down the hallway. Clean towels and washcloths are in the cupboard by the sink. Shampoo's in the shower."

AFTER SHOWERING and washing his hair, Garth pulled his shorts back on. His tank top was so dirty he dropped it in a corner, with his sweaty undershorts and prickly socks stuffed inside. If he'd known Dana better, he would have left his shorts there, too. His skin itched all over from the hay, bits and pieces having worked their way under the overalls. He'd even found some stuck in the stubble of his beard.

With the palm of his hand he rubbed his chin. He'd heard a man's beard grew faster when the old hormones were active. Well, his hormones had been working overtime since he'd met Dana. He wished he had a razor with him. He'd found one lying on the edge of the tub—a pink disposable—but only one, and he didn't think she'd appreciate his dulling the blade. After running a comb through his damp hair, he stepped back out into the hall-way.

It wasn't his day's growth of beard but the way the ma-terial of his shorts clung to certain parts of his anatomy that captured Dana's gaze. He obviously hadn't taken a cold shower. An urge to reach out and touch shocked her, and she could feel her cheeks growing red. Without think-ing about what she was doing, she handed him the can of Coke she'd been drinking from and hurried for the bath-room door.

Garth smiled. If he wasn't mistaken, Dana Allen was blushing. For a while he just stood where he was, listen-ing to her move about behind the closed door. Then the shower came on, and he realized he'd never offered to wash her back—a mistake he would soon rectify.

He walked over to the kitchen and put down the can of pop and was all the way back to the bathroom door when Dana began singing. He couldn't call himself a music critic, but he did prefer songs sung in tune. Still, there was a wholehearted enthusiasm in her singing he had to ad-mire. Actually there was a lot he admired about her, which he planned on telling her just as soon as he opened the door.

She'd locked it.

He stood staring at the doorknob, disappointed. Da-na's singing still filled the house. He had two choices: wait for her to come out, or break down the door. He decided to wait. Slowly he wandered into her living room.

The room was sparsely furnished, a sofa, easy chair and television taking up most of the space. Horse and rodeo magazines were piled high on the coffee table, and the walls were covered with pictures of Dana racing Wind-runner and the horse she called HoJo.

Garth wondered if she knew how his heart stopped every time she entered the arena. He'd been to six rodeos now and had seen two accidents. Neither had been serious, but they could have been. A horse going down spelled trouble. There were no guarantees that something wouldn't happen, and Dana was pushing herself too hard, taking chances. He sank down into her easy chair and stared out the window at the last rays of sunlight.

When Dana stepped out of the bathroom, she was wearing red shorts and a matching halter. Her wet hair had been brushed so it fell in long strands past her shoulders, and coral lipstick gave her mouth a lush, full appearance. Otherwise, she'd skipped makeup.

Garth rose from the chair and walked toward her. "Hi, beautiful."

"I don't know about beautiful, but I sure feel a lot cleaner." The way his eyes were devouring her made her skin go hot. She wouldn't let her gaze drop lower. Remembering how she'd reacted earlier, she felt it safer to keep her eyes on his face.

"I'm ready," he murmured, stopping directly in front of her.

"Ready?" Her pulse went crazy, her throat suddenly got very dry and breathing was impossible.

"For that rubdown you promised," he said quietly, smiling.

"Right." She tried to steady her heartbeat. "I'll get some liniment." If she could remember where she'd put it. Or if she could think of anything except how sexy his voice sounded or how good and manly he smelled. Dana started to turn away, but Garth wrapped his arms around her before she moved, bringing her close to his bare chest.

"I don't need any liniment, honey." He brushed a kiss over her forehead. "All I need is you." Tipping her head back, his mouth covered hers.

The heat of that afternoon was nothing compared to the internal thermal explosion Garth's kiss created. An exhilarating blast sent the blood zinging through her arteries. Her legs went weak, and she clung to his arms for support. "Oh, Garth, what your kisses do to me," she confessed shakily.

"And what yours do to me. Take me to your bedroom," he whispered against her mouth. "Let me make love to you."

Without another word, she stepped back, bringing him with her, toward her bedroom.

7

COOL BLUE was the feeling Garth got from Dana's bedroom. The quilted bedspread was blue and white, the carpeting was a blue plush and broad stripes of blue and yellow flowers covered the walls. A slight breeze billowed her blue nylon curtains into the room.

This was where she slept, where they would make love. He turned her and lifted her into his arms, carrying her the last few steps to her bed. There he laid her down on the quilt and stretched out beside her.

Dana kept her eyes on him, her insides churning with anticipation. It had been a long time since she'd made love. Would she be able to satisfy a man like Garth? He was so good-looking, so virile. He'd probably had many women; she'd known only one man.

"Garth—" she began, hesitant to say anything. "I'm not a virgin—I did live with a man for two years—but I'm not exactly what you'd call experienced."

"I don't care." It didn't matter. He knew instinctively that what they were about to share would be unique. Lightly he touched a finger to her cheek. Her skin was so soft. He traced the contour of her face, then the line of her nose and her lips.

His eyes were a smoky blue, warning of the fire smoldering just below the surface. Dana stared into them. She was mesmerized by his gentle touch, her heart lodged in her throat.

"I like you, Dana Allen," he said softly. "And I want you more than I've ever wanted a woman."

"I want you, too." Her voice was shaky and a shiver ran down her spine.

They leaned toward each other and their lips touched. It was a tentative kiss, hesitant and short-lived. Immediately afterward, each drew back. Dana closed her eyes and tried to slow the accelerated rate of her breathing.

"Think we can get rid of this?"

Not waiting for an answer, Garth sat up and leaned over her, pushing her hair aside to find the neck straps of her halter. When the two strings were loosened the material drooped forward, just barely exposing her small breasts. Moving his hands lower, he released the remaining tie and slipped off the halter.

Again he stretched out beside her, pressed a kiss to her lips, then gently touched her breasts. Her nipples were already erect and he played with the taut buds, rubbing first one then the other between his fingers and thumb. He liked the way her body responded. She was growing larger before his eyes. Covering one breast with a hand, he leaned close and kissed her lips. His tongue coaxed, and she opened her mouth.

As his fingers caressed her soft skin, their tongues parried playfully. Tension was changing to desire, and her body was becoming warm and pliant. His lips never parting from hers, he pulled her over onto him and she adjusted her position, holding the contact but bringing her knees up to hug his thighs.

When they finally took a break, it was for air. Loving the heady feeling his kisses gave her, she laughed. "You take my breath away, sir."

"I'll give you something in return."

"Think so?" Seductively running her hands over his chest, she moved her fingers through the thick mat of dark hair. She was losing her hesitancy and impishly pulled a few of the curly tendrils. Then her fingers traveled downward, over his navel and on to the elastic waistband of his shorts. She felt him suck in a breath and knew she had two choices—over or under.

She chose over, her hands sliding across the smooth cotton of his shorts, coming close to but never quite touching the expanded outline of his manhood. He continued holding his breath, and she smiled, knowing exactly what she was doing. "Have any hay down your pants?" she asked teasingly.

"Maybe you should check and see. I wouldn't want to get any on this beautiful quilt."

"No, that wouldn't be good, would it?" But she didn't pull down his shorts. Instead her hands traveled to the safer territory of his legs.

"Chicken." He chuckled and reached up to bring her back down against him, pressing her breasts against his bare chest and intimately aligning their hips.

Kiss after kiss raised his level of passion. His hands slid down and under her shorts, his need growing stronger. The skimpy pieces of material separating their bodies were annoying nuisances—nuisances to be removed. Rolling her to the side, he finished undressing her.

Within minutes neither wore any clothing. Dana pulled back the quilt and stretched out on the cotton sheet. Sitting beside her, Garth gazed down at her naked body. "Beautiful," he said again, meaning it. She wasn't beautiful in the classic sense of the word, but to him every part of her seemed perfect. His hands touched the velvety skin of her breasts. Her rose-colored areolas were a contrast to the creamy white flesh, her nipples were proudly erect.

She sighed, the sound almost a purr. His eyes were devouring her, and she felt warm all over. Reaching out, she touched a pale scar on his thigh. Another started at his hip and stretched around to his back. "At last I get to see your scars." She sat up and twisted her body to check behind him. The one she'd seen before ran from his tailbone halfway up his back.

"And all the king's men put Humpty Dumpty back together again."

"I'm glad they did."

She sat back, looking at him in a way that made him proud to be a man. "So am I," he said quietly and laid her back down on the bed, his mouth covering hers.

While she ran her fingers through his hair, ruffling it more than usual and loving its luxuriant feel, his hands caressed her body with whisper-soft touches, seeking and learning the places that pleased her most. And then he touched her between her legs—ever so lightly—and she took in a quick gasp, her hands stilling.

"Are you all right?" he asked.

"Yes." She felt wonderful.

His fingertips moved over the sensitive area. "Do you like that?"

"Yes," she gasped again, unsure how long she could take what he was doing to her.

"Good." His finger moved in a sweet, rhythmic motion, stimulating an elemental pleasure. Leaning close, he kissed her, his mouth holding her pinned to the bed.

Nevertheless she was soaring, spinning. His touch was becoming a sweet torture. She wanted him with her, inside her. Moaning, she tried to tell him, but his kisses blocked the words. His finger moved into her, and Dana grasped his hair. He had to stop...she was going to...going to—

Her body convulsed, waves of pleasure ending the torture. He murmured sweet, encouraging words and she clung to him, shocked by the height of her response. Then slowly, delightfully, she floated back down and a sweet lassitude invaded her body.

Finally Garth sat back and smiled down at her. He knew he'd brought her pleasure, and he loved the lambent glow in her eyes when she raised her lids and looked up at him.

She was shaken by what had happened. She hadn't expected him to bring her to a climax that way—or so quickly—and a part of her still ached for him. "Aren't you...?" She wasn't quite sure how to ask. "Will you...?"

"Yes, I will," he promised softly, then began to look around for where he'd dropped his shorts. "But first, I need to find something."

Dana was sure she knew what he was looking for and touched his arm. "It's okay. I'm protected. That weekend you went with me to the rodeos, I decided I'd better be prepared—just in case."

He stopped his search. "Didn't you think I'd keep my word?"

She stared at his virile body and knew what she'd been afraid of. "I wasn't sure I'd stick to my decision."

"So you became Miss Don't-Touch-Me." He smiled, then moved slowly, carefully settling himself over her. "Well, I'm going to touch you now, my sweet." He kissed her shoulder, then her neck, his knees spreading her legs apart. "I told you we'd make love—" his mouth brushed over hers, his words a mere whisper "—someday."

His first thrust took him deep into her, and he groaned, weeks of frustration at last finding relief. A sense of completeness enveloped him, and he knew what he was feeling was more than just a physical satisfaction.

Dana closed her eyes and also felt complete. Something had been missing in her life. She hadn't even known it, but now she'd found it. Garth had become a part of her—physically and mentally. She held on to his shoulders and wrapped her legs around him. Never would she let him go.

He began to move his hips, long-suppressed desire setting a rapid pace. His breathing quickly became ragged, his body hot and damp. "Yes, oh yes," he chanted, wanting to hold on to the sweetness of the moment, but knowing it couldn't be held.

She gripped his arms and arched her back, taking him deeper, her own body surprising her with its ready response. She'd never had more than one climax a night when making love with John, and even those were a rarity. But each powerful thrust of Garth's hips was taking her into a realm of ecstasy. Clinging to him, she let the feelings come. She heard Garth's rapturous cry, then found her own release.

THE TELEPHONE RANG.

Dana cringed and closed her eyes. Who would be calling at this hour?

Again it rang.

She didn't want to talk to anyone, didn't want to get up and leave Garth's side. Not now, not when the world seemed so perfect.

Again . . . and again . . . and again came the insistent, nerve-grating summons.

Every time the shrill sound reached the bedroom, Dana tensed. She just wasn't the kind who could ignore a telephone call. She hated the not knowing. And this caller was so persistent.

Six rings. Seven.

Dana swore and pushed herself away from Garth. "I can't stand it any longer," she confessed.

The telephone was still ringing when she reached it. She hadn't even paused to grab a robe, and as soon as she heard the voice on the other end of the line, she inched back into the hallway, away from the kitchen and living room. She didn't want to be in a position where she could be seen through a window.

"Mom, you're home. How was the fair today?"

She listened to her mother's glowing report on how much money her brother's calves had brought at the 4-H auction. Then she smiled. "Why, yes, Mom, it did ring a long time, didn't it." She wasn't going to try to come up with an excuse.

Dana leaned back against the wall. She could see into the bedroom. Garth was still lying on his side, naked, his head propped up on one hand so he could watch her. He looked like a Greek statue—muscular and nicely proportioned. A hairy statue, she decided. But not *too* hairy. Just right. Everything about Garth seemed just right tonight.

"What, Mom?" Dana realized she'd missed her mother's question.

Garth grinned, clearly aware that she'd been eyeing him and not listening. She made a face back.

"I'll ask him," she answered. "Garth, they're having blueberry pie up at the house. Do you want to go up and have some?"

He shook his head, motioning with a finger for her to come back to him.

She knew what he wanted. She wanted it, too. "No, I've got dessert here," she told her mother. "He says that's all he wants."

Garth nodded enthusiastically, still grinning.

"Ah—we're having, ah, having—ah—ice cream," Dana stammered. She hadn't expected her mother to ask what she'd be serving.

"Yes, I know he loves blueberry pie." She rolled her eyes toward the ceiling. Her mother was pushing this hospitality bit too far. "I think he's tired, Mom. He just wants to finish dinner and head home. He's not used to this kind of work, remember."

However, her city boy was no softy. Another point in his favor. Lately Garth had been racking up a lot of points in his favor.

"No, Mom..."

She thought she'd never get back to Garth's side. "I should have let it keep ringing," she mumbled, sitting down on the bed.

"Then she'd probably have sent Danny over to see why you didn't answer."

"Probably." Dana chuckled. "That might have been interesting." Lightly he ran his fingertips up and down her back, and she remembered her earlier promise. "Ready for that back rub?"

"Actually, I kinda liked it when you rubbed my front."

"No dice. Roll over, mister. I promised a back rub, and that's what you're getting."

"If the lady insists." He rolled onto his stomach, grinning. She'd be rubbing his front soon. He was sure of that.

Starting at his shoulders, Dana worked in a downward direction, moving the heels of her hands in circles and pressing hard. He groaned in pleasure and closed his eyes. Her hands weren't as soft as some that had caressed his body, but the pleasure she was bringing his strained muscles was more welcome than any other touch he'd known. She kneaded the muscles of his lower back and he sighed. As far as he was concerned, she could keep this up all night.

Dana grinned to herself when her hands reached his bottom. It hadn't been that long ago that she'd been tempted to reach out and give the back of his shorts a little pat. Lightly she patted the solid muscles, then gave one cheek a small pinch.

"What's that for?" he asked, opening his eyes and lifting his head slightly.

"For being such a temptation. Feel better?"

"Part of me does." Having a massage given by a naked woman was the ultimate men's fantasy. Her rubdown had relaxed some muscles, but others were reacting in an opposite fashion. "I heard you tell your mother we were going to have dessert here."

"And just what would you like for dessert?" she asked, pretty sure she knew.

"Something sweet and succulent." He rolled over, pulling her down beside him. "Something we could both enjoy."

"I lied, I don't have any ice cream. Besides, we don't like the same kind."

"I don't want ice cream." His hands began to caress her body, and he brushed his lips over hers.

"And just what do you want?" She put her arms around his neck and kissed him back.

"You." Garth groaned. "Oh, Dana, I can't get enough of you." He kissed her cheeks and eyelids, nipped an earlobe and nibbled the length of her neck. The taste of her soft skin excited him. He wanted to absorb all of her. With a smile and a low, guttural moan, he positioned himself over her.

It was after midnight when Dana closed her eyes and slipped under the veil of sleep. Vaguely she was aware of Garth drawing away, of strong hands moving her and a sheet being pulled over her shoulders. That was all she remembered. The next morning she found herself in bed—alone.

Garth hadn't said anything about coming back out Sunday, so Dana was surprised when, just before noon, she looked down from the hayloft to see his tan Bronco pull up. He stepped out dressed in jeans and a long-sleeved shirt, looking ready to go to work. And she was even more surprised when three burly teenagers also climbed out of the Bronco.

"I called a friend of mine who coaches the high-school football team," Garth explained, standing by the hay wagon, her father having called a break. "I told him I needed some workers and he provided me with three. Said it would help get them into shape. Chet. Steve. Bruce. This is Mr. Allen, Dana and—" he pointed to the two boys still up in the loft "—Gordon and Paul."

The three husky football players nodded. Dana noticed they were also appropriately dressed for working with the hay.

"All they need are gloves," said Garth. He was learning.

"Call me Dan," her father insisted and headed for the house to find some gloves.

"You're just full of surprises, aren't you?" said Dana, her eyes moving from Garth's head to his toes, then back again. It seemed strange to see him in clothes again; stranger, yet, to know how well they knew each other's bodies.

"Just trying to find a way to get you to myself for a while. Think you'd like to have dinner at my place tonight?"

"If we're done in time." And she hoped they were. Just being near him made her ache for his touch.

"We'll be done in time—" he chuckled "—if I have to cancel all breaks."

"And you were so nice yesterday." She saw her father heading back toward the barn and gave Garth's rear end a pat. "Come on, Simon Legree, let's get the slaves to work."

They did finish in time. Garth drove the boys back to town and Dana left the farm an hour later, driving her own truck. She'd taken time for a shower, and then—for the first time since she'd met him—put on a dress. The dress stayed on through the meal he prepared, then ended up next to his clothes on the floor by his bed. It was late in the evening before he asked the one question she'd hoped he wouldn't. "How do you like my apartment?"

"I don't. Garth, how can you stand having people look in your living-room window every time they walk by?"

"If I don't want them to look in, I close the blinds," he answered matter-of-factly.

"Then you can't look out. And the noise." There was a stereo on the second floor that had blared out rock-and-roll music until after dinner. "I hate apartments—all apartments."

"It's always quiet around here by seven o'clock. Those are the rules." It bothered him that she didn't like his place. Her reaction was so vehement, there had to be a reason. "When you lived with that other man, did you live in an apartment?"

Dana nodded and stared at the bedroom ceiling.

"Tell me about him."

She glanced at Garth, her eyes meeting with his, then returned her gaze to the ceiling. "About who?"

"You know who. The man you lived with."

She continued staring at the ceiling, not sure if she wanted to talk about John.

"You loved him?"

"Yes," she said finally, the word a sibilant sigh. *Love* was a strange word. It had so many different meanings. She loved winning a barrel race. She loved her family. And she had loved John, once.

"For two years?" It had to have been a serious love affair to have lasted that long. He wondered why it had ended.

"Actually, my life centered around John for three years." In many ways it now seemed like a wasted three years. "I was just finishing college when we met at a party. The funny thing is, I think he was attracted to me because I wasn't like the other girls there. I was more natural, he said. Unsophisticated. Then, for the next three years, he tried to change me."

Garth gently turned her head until he could see into her dark eyes. "I don't want to change you, Dana," he said quietly.

She managed a smile, then it grew broader. "I hope not. I've grown quite stubborn in my old age."

"So I've noticed. Tell me more about him."

It was easier now. "There's not a lot to tell. His name was . . . is John Burton. He's an engineer and he has a mother who's a terror." Dana actually laughed, remembering. "Oh, what a terror!

"He considered my family a bunch of hicks. They didn't like him, either. He tried to 'refine' me—those were his words—but in the end he dumped me. His parting dig was, 'You can take a girl out of the country, but you can't take the country out of the girl.' Now, what about you?"

"No problem." He smiled and leaned toward her to kiss her forehead. "I don't want to take anything out of you. I like you fine, just as you are."

"Well, thank you." She was flattered, but not so gullible she believed every word. "But, I mean, tell me about your great love."

"I've never had one." He wasn't really sure about that. He might be lying beside the great love of his life right now.

"Never?" That surprised Dana.

"I was too busy being rebellious when I was younger, and too busy building up a business later. You're looking at a virgin."

"Right." She laughed and reached down to touch him. Immediately he responded. "And next you're going to tell me I seduced you."

"That's right." Pulling her on top of him, he fit her hips to his. "And I think you're going to do it again."

OVER THE NEXT four days she saw as much of Garth as she could. There was no time for lovemaking, but he took her to lunch every day and she even stayed in town late Tuesday, deciding it wouldn't hurt Windrunner to have one night off. Garth took her to dinner and a play. It was the first time she'd been to the theater in over three years, and she had to admit she enjoyed it. Then Wednesday night Garth came out and helped with her handicapped class. He truly seemed to like working with the kids.

She had Friday off. There were three rodeos that weekend in as many states. Garth offered to go with her and she willingly agreed. She wanted to be with him. Two nights of lovemaking had merely whetted her sexual appetite. She wanted more of the sweetness they'd shared.

Atlanta, Michigan, was the first stop and as soon as Dana had finished competing, she loaded Windrunner up and they were on the road, headed for Illinois. Spelling each other with the driving, they both got some sleep en route.

In New Windsor, Garth insisted they get a motel room, and for once Dana didn't argue. She told herself she was going along with his suggestion because she was tired; yet, when she stepped out of the shower, she felt keenly awake and alert, and seeing the glint in Garth's eyes, she knew they wouldn't be getting much sleep.

Saturday afternoon, Dana saw Sharon. "Good heavens, are you sure you're not carrying twins?"

Sharon, with her abdomen protruding far ahead of her, rubbed the small of her back. Circles shadowed her eyes and Dana was sure her friend wasn't getting any more sleep than she was.

"The doctor insists there's only one. Cody swears I swallowed a watermelon."

Dana chuckled.

"You look good." Sharon cocked her head to the side, studying her, then smiled. "Garth keeping you happy?"

"You're so sure it's Garth?"

Sharon nodded. "I may have missed a few rodeos you've been at, but I keep tabs. I've heard quite a few cowgirls talking about your broad-shouldered, blue-eyed man. You'd better keep a rope on him. Where's he now?"

Dana glanced toward her truck and horse trailer, then over at the rodeo arena. Garth had been around just a while before. Then she saw him, talking to Cody. "Over there." She pointed in the direction of Sharon's rig. "Talking to the broad-shouldered man you put a rope on."

Sharon studied the two men for a moment, then looked back at Dana. "So when are you two getting married?"

"You're jumping the barrier with that idea. We're just . . . good friends," Dana insisted.

"How good?"

"Nosy, aren't you." Dana wasn't upset. Long ago she'd gotten used to Sharon's forthright questions. "To tell you the truth, I don't know. Physically—" she nodded "—good."

Sharon grinned. "And that explains the glow."

"Yes, but that's really all we have in common. We're still very different. He's still a city boy and I'm still a country girl. I know he'd never move out to the country, just as I know I'd never move into the city."

"So, take it one day at a time. That's how I'm doin' it." She patted her belly. "One day Junior says, 'Sit down Mom, take it easy.' So I do. The next I feel great, ready to hop in the saddle again."

"I notice you're not going to as many rodeos." Dana had missed her friend's presence and encouragement.

"I'll probably be going to even fewer. The doctor wants me to stay off my feet as much as possible."

"You won't be going to Sparta, then?" The Klein Rodeo in Sparta, Michigan, was the largest rodeo held in the United States on Labor Day weekend. Its payout was often enough to cinch the regional standings that ended two weeks later.

"Oh, I'll be there. Wouldn't miss that one. Good luck this afternoon."

BUT LUCK WASN'T with Dana that afternoon—or the next. By the end of the weekend Connie Birch was in the lead again, and Dana was worried. She'd made errors while running the pattern—silly mistakes that had cost her fractions of a second—and Windrunner had lacked his usual drive. She was sure the lax training schedule she'd followed the week before, and her lack of sleep—due to her extracurricular activities—were part of the problem. Garth was taking up too much of her time.

Not that she wanted to cut back on the time she spent with him. It seemed as if the more they were together, the more she wanted to be with him. He'd turned into an addiction, albeit a marvelous one.

The next week Dana tried to find time for everything and everyone. She handled her job with her usual efficiency, got the farm's accounts up-to-date so all the creditors were happy, gave her weekly lesson to her handicapped students, worked Windrunner on the pattern until she was sure he hadn't picked up any bad habits, had his feet trimmed and shoes reset, then loped and trotted him for miles to bring him back to the peak of conditioning.

Garth was the one who was given the least of her time. He did manage to talk her into having lunch with him twice, but she had to turn down his dinner invitations. And even when he came out to the farm, the only time she could really talk to him was during her lesson on Wednesday evening. There was no time when they could make love, and she knew he was getting frustrated. So was she. But she didn't know what to do about it.

She almost thought he wouldn't be going to the rodeos with her that weekend. When he saw the distances she had to drive, he voiced his disapproval. "It's ridiculous. You drive too far, get too little sleep, eat poorly and drink too many of those Cokes. Dana, you're pushing yourself too hard, pushing your horse and your truck. One day Windrunner's going to quit and that Ford's going to fall apart around you."

"I know it's in bad shape," she admitted. The old Ford might already have given up if Garth hadn't been constantly tinkering with it. He'd reduced the shimmy in the wheel, tightened a dozen loose nuts and bolts, kept the oil level up and even spent one evening putting on new brake shoes. "Just a little longer, then maybe I'll have a new truck."

"Maybe." He spit out the word. "And maybe, instead, you'll end up putting your truck and trailer in a ditch because you're too tired to stay on the road. I shouldn't even go with you this weekend, Dana. I've got a business to run."

"Then don't come." She felt guilty as it was. She knew he had worries of his own. They were starting construction of his new garage. He should be concentrating on that, not on her. "I can find someone to buddy up with."

"Who? Anne?"

"Maybe."

He snorted. Anne had made it to a few rodeos and Garth had met her. He didn't think much of the woman, though it was evident that Anne was impressed with him and would have been more than willing to share his bed. "She'd probably desert you midtrip for a cowboy. I'll say it again: Dana Allen, you're pushing yourself too hard."

"I'm not pushing myself hard enough. Connie's ahead. If I don't go to these rodeos, she's going to be even further ahead. If I don't win that twenty thousand, we lose the farm." Tears formed in her eyes and she fought them back. Dammit all, she wasn't going to go and get emotional. Turning away from him, she spit out her decision: "You take care of your business. I'll take care of mine."

Garth stared at her rigid shoulders. He should do just exactly that. In Kalamazoo his foreman had been complaining all week; in Battle Creek the builder had been screwing up. And he knew he was tired. Driving to Clay and back every night was telling on him. He needed to stay home, catch up on his reading, book work, and rest. But more than all the reasons put together, he needed to be with Dana. "I'll go with you," he decided.

By Sunday night, he wished he hadn't.

8

MURPHY'S LAW ruled the weekend. Anything that could go wrong, did. The trip started with a bang—a tire blowing out that nearly put truck and trailer in a ditch—and ended with a downpour that made driving difficult and unloading Windrunner a soaking experience. Halfway to the barn, a bolt of lightning hit a tree in the distant woods, and the gelding jerked to the side, bringing a hoof solidly down on Garth's shoe.

"Damn!" Garth swore and instinctively struck out.

Windrunner made another short hop—off Garth's foot and back toward Dana—the whites of his eyes showing and his nostrils flaring.

"He's upset enough. You don't have to hit him!" she yelled.

"What am I supposed to do, let him stand on my foot?" With rain running down his face and his wet shirt sticking to his skin, he pulled open the barn door.

"If you'd wear boots instead of—"

Dana didn't finish. Leading Windrunner past Garth to his box stall, she tried to remember that they were both tired and that Garth had just driven two hundred miles—staring at headlights through a rain-streaked windshield, the wipers barely doing their job. He'd driven so she could sleep. She should be grateful for his help, not jumping down his throat. If he wanted to wear tennis shoes, that was his business.

He watched her wipe Windrunner down, remove the horse's leg wraps, check his water and bring his hay. Garth wished she'd pay as much attention to him. Perhaps he was being ridiculous, but he sometimes wondered if she even noticed his presence. All weekend, all she'd talked about was tighter turns and faster sprints. Even when they finally managed to find a little time together, he'd questioned whether he really had her full attention.

The problem was she completely held *his* attention. Even now, as tired as he was, her feminine curves enticed him. Her wet, ruffled blouse was molded to her breasts and her gaberdine dress pants hugged her slender hips. A vision of Dana lying naked on a bed brought an invigorating surge of warmth to his limbs. No matter how many times they made love, he wanted more. Holding her in his arms, being a part of her, was habit-forming.

The last few miles to the farm, he'd thought about what to do when they arrived. He knew he couldn't spend the night with her; he needed to get back to his apartment, finish some forms and get some sleep. He'd decided the best thing to do was kiss her good-night and head for home. But as he looked at her, his thoughts were changing. Maybe he couldn't spend the night, but he could spend an hour or two. Those forms on his kitchen table would wait. Another need was growing more important. *Hurry up and get that horse taken care of,* he silently willed.

"Good boy," Dana crooned against Windrunner's neck, giving him several solid pats. "You tried. Maybe we didn't come in first, but you beat Connie's horse. We can still win. I know we can."

Windrunner nickered and impatiently tossed his head, inching toward the hay manger.

"He's more interested in filling his stomach than in praise," Garth called to her. "Tell him good-night and let's go get out of these wet clothes."

Dana released her hold on the gelding, and Windrunner moved straight to his feed. She stared at her horse for a second, then turned and left the stall, closing the door. Slowly she walked toward Garth, her eyes moving over his wet jeans and polo shirt. She wasn't sure why, but tonight it irked her that he didn't dress like a cowboy. Sometimes she felt he was blatantly trying to prove he was different.

Different. The word rattled around in her head. Yes, he was different. Most of the time that was what made him special. Right now, it was simply one more thing bothering her.

Today, everything was bothering her—from the taste of her Coke to the unexpected rain. The truth was, she was scared. Time was running out and she wasn't where she'd hoped to be. Connie was only ahead by two hundred fifty dollars, but she was still ahead, and Windrunner was off form—or maybe she was. Sharon had said she might be trying too hard. The problem was, she didn't know what else to do.

"Tired?" Garth asked, slipping his arm around her shoulders as they walked toward the barn door.

"Beat." It was an understatement.

From the back of her truck he pulled out their two tote bags, then together they dashed through the pelting rain for her house. Garth merely noted in passing that his Bronco still looked all right. He opened her door, snapped on the lights, stood back and let her go in first.

"Thank goodness it wasn't raining like this this afternoon," she said, immediately taking off her hat. Raindrops slid from its clear plastic cover onto the entryway's linoleum.

"They'd have had to cancel the rodeo if it'd rained like this, wouldn't they?" Garth dropped their bags on the floor and shook his head, sending a spray of droplets into the air.

Dana smiled. He made her think of a dog straight from a bath. "Rodeos go on, rain or shine. Sometimes they're delayed a bit, but I've never had one canceled."

"You've got to be kidding." He ran his fingers through his hair, but when he was finished, it was in even more disarray than usual.

"No."

"You'd ride in this?"

"If I was scheduled to ride, yes."

"Wouldn't that be dangerous? I mean, couldn't Windrunner slip?" He stared at her slender profile. She looked younger than ever, tonight . . . vulnerable. He wanted to protect her, wanted to ease her burden, wanted—

"I don't like running when the arena's wet, but we all have to, sometime or another. Want anything before you leave?" she asked, stepping into the kitchen.

'Maybe." He smiled. He wanted her.

"I could fix you some instant coffee."

"No, no coffee." Coming up behind, Garth wrapped his arms around her and drew her back. Her rain-soaked blouse felt cold against his skin and the rigid peaks of her nipples pressed hard against his forearms. "Why don't we just get out of these wet clothes, take a hot shower and crawl into bed?"

Dana leaned back, enjoying his embrace. His suggestion did sound good. The one time they'd had a chance to get together that weekend hadn't really been the best. She'd been too preoccupied with the run she had coming up. Now it was all behind her, and she could relax and enjoy the pleasure he offered. Simply feeling his strong arms around her was doing funny things to her insides.

Then, almost by habit, she glanced at the clock on the wall.

It was past eleven. At five in the morning her alarm would go off. Even if she went to sleep right now, she'd get less than six hours sleep. Not enough. Her boss was beginning to question the circles under her eyes, and as generous as he'd been in allowing her to split up her vacation time to go to the rodeos, she owed him an alert mind and rested body. Reluctantly she made her decision. "Not tonight, Garth."

Immediately he let her go and stepped back. "Any particular reason why?" He felt defensive. She had, after all, been a less than attentive partner the last time they'd made love. As much as he hated to admit it, she might be growing tired of him, might not share the feelings he had.

"I'm exhausted." She turned and faced him. In his eyes she saw his disbelief. "Really, I am. I don't know about you, but if I don't get some sleep, I'm not going to be worth anything tomorrow."

She was right. In fact, he was probably being overly sensitive because he was tired. A good night's sleep would do them both good. "Okay, I'll give you a rain check." Considering the weather, it seemed appropriate. "Tomorrow night, after work, come to my apartment and I'll fix you dinner. And—" he smiled, sensuously "—later we can share some dessert."

"Ice cream?" She ran her tongue teasingly over her lips, then laughed at the pained expression that crossed his face. "What flavor?"

"Hmm, how's Ecstasy's Delight sound?" He took a step back toward her. "Sure we don't have time for a sample tonight?"

Grinning, she shook her head. "I'm sure. I'm also afraid we're going to have to wait longer than tomorrow. No go on dinner at your apartment. I need to come home after work and train Windrunner. His timing just doesn't seem right."

"Windrunner!" The horse's name exploded out of Garth's mouth. "I am so damned tired of playing second fiddle to that horse!"

Dana was taken aback by the anger in his voice and the rigid line of his jaw. But only for a second. Then her own chin lifted and a dark fire blazed from her eyes. "Garth Roberts, the first time I met you I told you I didn't have time for a relationship, not now. But no, you wouldn't listen. You followed me to St. Charles, came out here to the farm, seduced me—"

"Seduced you?" he challenged.

"All right, maybe that's not the right word. I'll agree I've been a willing participant in the lovemaking we've shared. However—" she refused to be sidetracked "—the point is, from the very beginning, I told you I had to concentrate on winning the money we need for the mortgage. The only way I can do that is make sure I'm the best. And to be the best, I have to train and condition that horse of mine."

"In other words, I've been a pest." He looked toward her bedroom. "You participated, but it would have been better if I'd never bothered you. Is that right?"

He was twisting her words around, and that upset her. "Of course not. I didn't say you'd been a pest. You've helped a lot around here—with the hay, driving with me to all these rodeos."

"A good old buddy."

"More than that," she insisted. "I . . . I like you."

"How nice." His tone was cold and sarcastic. "You like me. But not enough to spend an evening with me at my place."

Dana bristled. "Garth, I explained why. Besides, I hate going to your apartment. I feel confined there."

"Oh, so now you don't like where I live! In other words, I can drive all the way out here, hang around hoping you'll spare me a few minutes of your precious time, maybe swim in your mucky, weedy pond, but you can't spend a couple hours or a night at my place."

She closed her eyes and chewed on her lower lip. Damn him, why was he doing this to her, twisting her words all around? Why now? Why tonight? She didn't want to fight. She just wanted him to leave and let her get some sleep.

"You keep telling me we're different. Well, maybe we are," he agreed vehemently. "I feel that when two people care for each other they should share in each other's life. I'm willing to share in yours, Dana, but you don't seem to want to share any part of mine." Turning on one heel, he walked to the door, picked up his tote bag, then paused to look back.

She was watching him, her dark eyes wide with surprise.

"I like you, too, Dana—a lot. If you ever decide you're willing to meet me halfway, give me a call. Just remember, though, I'm a selfish man. I won't be second in your life."

THAT HE WAS GONE—out of her life—didn't really set in until the end of the week. Dana didn't expect to hear from him Monday night, but she wouldn't have been surprised if he'd called or driven out to the farm Tuesday. And Wednesday she really expected him to come to help with the handicapped kids. Garth had thoroughly enjoyed working with them, and they loved him. In fact, it was hard for her to explain to Katie why Garth wasn't around, and she could tell that Billy and Cindy missed him.

By Thursday a restless uneasiness took over her mind. She couldn't concentrate on anything. When the telephone at work rang, she jumped, her heartbeat accelerating. Then, when the call turned out to be business oriented, a wave of depression washed over her. At home it was worse. Friends and salesmen alike were abruptly put off. She simply couldn't talk to anyone—not when she wanted the caller to be Garth.

She thought heading out for a string of rodeos would help, but she made the mistake of asking Anne to buddy up with her. All the woman wanted to do was to talk about Garth. Although Anne gave her sympathy that things hadn't worked out, Dana had the feeling Anne was just waiting to get back home so she could call him.

Fine, she thought. *Anne's welcome to him.* But Dana knew she was lying to herself.

In barely six weeks, Garth had become a part of her life. She missed his quiet strength, his laughter and wisdom. She missed the stubble of beard he was forever battling, the glint of desire in his smoky blue eyes and the feel of his body against and inside of hers. She hadn't wanted to get involved, but the truth was, she had.

Saturday afternoon, waiting for the rodeo to start, she looked toward the stands. In the shadows of the overhang, Dana saw the broad shoulders that had become so familiar to her. And when, his back still toward the arena, he ran his fingers through his dark hair as he always did, her pulse quickened. He'd come to see her. He couldn't stay away. He'd come to watch her run.

Then the man turned to face the arena, and her hopes died. It wasn't Garth.

Sunday she returned home determined to put Garth out of her mind. They were too different. Why prolong the inevitable? He'd done her a service by walking out on her. She'd done just fine before she met him, and she'd do just fine again.

By Thursday night, she realized she was wrong. She wasn't doing fine at all. She couldn't eat and she couldn't sleep. Leaning against the railing of the pasture, she watched Windrunner graze. In the morning she'd be loading up and heading for the first in a series of rodeos. It was Labor Day weekend, and Sunday afternoon she'd be competing at Sparta. With a little luck she'd regain her lead over Connie Birch. A mere twenty dollars now separated their winnings, and Dana could tell that the strain of competition was beginning to tell on the fourteen-year-old.

The problem was, Dana was also suffering from strain—emotional strain. Her preoccupation with Garth was affecting everything she did—her work, her daily life and her riding. The mortgage, the farm, even winning barrel races, all seemed inconsequential. She'd lost something more important.

Pushing herself away from the fence, she walked toward her house. Garth was right. She'd tried to play the game her way. Selfishly she'd made him come to her, live in her world. She'd been so preoccupied with her problems, she hadn't thought about any he might be facing.

Maybe she hated his apartment, but the time she'd gone to dinner and a play with him she'd enjoyed herself. There had to be other things they could share and enjoy. Also, a few hours a week in his apartment wouldn't be a commitment to live there. She needed to bend a little.

Her hand was shaking when she picked up the telephone. Listening to his phone ring, she crossed her fingers and chewed on her lower lip, silently counting. On the sixth ring an answering machine came on. "Hi. Sorry, I can't come to the phone right now, if—"

Dana hung up. She couldn't stand hearing his voice, yet knowing he wasn't there. She dialed Roberts's Auto Center. He'd been there that first night they met, working late. Perhaps...

After the sixth ring, an answering machine came on there, too, and she hung up.

Fifteen minutes later she tried his apartment again. And again the answering machine came on.

She hadn't had anything to eat since lunch, and she wandered into the kitchen. Logic told her she should be hungry, but the knots in her stomach warned that any and all food would be rejected. Instead she opened a Coke and took a swallow.

In the living room she turned on the television, jumped from channel to channel, then stopped at a baseball game. Her father would be sitting in his big easy chair, up at the farmhouse, watching this game. Garth was a dyed-in-the-wool Tigers fan. Why wasn't he home watching? Dana stared at the screen. It took a few seconds before she realized it wasn't the Tigers playing, but two other teams. Then the ongoing scores of the American League games were listed and announced. It was a home game for the Tigers, and they were ahead. "That should make you happy," she murmured, and snapped off the television. Fifteen minutes later, she tried Garth's number again.

FRIDAY MORNING Dana went up to the farmhouse to say goodbye before she headed for the first rodeo on her schedule. In case of an emergency, she always let her folks know roughly where she'd be each day she was away. Her mother was fixing breakfast, her father was out in the barn and her brother was still asleep.

"We might try to get up to Sparta Sunday and watch you run," her mother said, cracking eggs into a bowl.

"I'm just hoping it doesn't rain. The weather report wasn't very encouraging."

"If it does rain, I doubt we'll go. You know how your dad hates to drive that truck if the weather's not just perfect."

Dana nodded and picked up a piece of toast from the plate on the counter. She hadn't eaten at all the night before and knew she should put something in her stomach. Taking a bite, she watched her mother add milk to the eggs. The toast, she could handle. Scrambled eggs didn't sound the least bit appetizing.

"Too bad you couldn't find someone to share the driving with this weekend," Nancy Allen commented, picking up a whisk to beat the mixture.

"I decided haulin' on my own was better than buddying up with Anne again. That gal's not interested in barrel racing. She's interested in cowboy hustling."

Her mother chuckled, then looked at Dana, her expression serious. "You still haven't heard from Garth?"

The toast turned to cardboard in Dana's mouth, her stomach twisting into a knot. She swallowed hard, took a second to compose herself, then answered. "I tried calling him last night. Several times. All I ever got was an answering machine. He's probably already found another woman and forgotten me."

"You really think so?"

Dana stared out the kitchen window. "I don't know what to think."

"He didn't strike me as a man who hopped from woman to woman."

From the window she could see her place, and she recalled the evenings Garth had come to visit, the times they'd spent in her bedroom. He'd told her he hadn't been with a woman for months, and she'd believed him. She still believed him. "No, I don't think he's the type."

"Then don't jump to conclusions. Did you try him this morning?"

"No." Dana looked back at her mother. "It seemed too early."

"Did you ever leave a message for him?"

"No."

Nancy Allen shook her head, then nodded toward the hallway, where the telephone was. "Go give him a call now. If he cares for you as much as I think he does, it won't matter if you wake him. And if the man's not home, leave a message. It's time you stopped walking around like a zombie."

"I'm not walking around like a zombie," argued Dana. She wasn't sure she was ready to try Garth again. If he wasn't home, she'd be left wondering.

"Well, you look close to one. You've got circles under your eyes and I bet you've lost ten pounds in the past two weeks."

"You're sure flattering."

"Go call him," her mother insisted.

Dana hesitated, then shrugged and walked into the hallway. Picking up the phone, she dialed the number that was now so familiar. On the sixth ring the same click she'd heard over and over again the night before told her Garth wasn't home. "Hi. Sorry—"

She hung up.

Staring at the telephone, she chewed on her lower lip. She really should get going. She had a long drive ahead of her. The knot tightened in her stomach. She did feel like a zombie—the living dead. What was she going to do?

Dana picked up the phone again. At the sound of the tone, she left her message.

IT WOULD HAVE BEEN better if she could have talked to Garth, but Dana felt she'd at least taken a step. She'd told him she'd be glad to meet him halfway and asked him to call her Tuesday. Now all she wanted to do was get through the long weekend.

Friday night she did well. Her time held up for first place. That, plus the day money, would cover her expenses and give her a little cushion. Saturday she had another fast time and was sure she'd be in the money. However, the important rodeo was Sunday. It was the points from that one that would count toward the regional championship.

She drove onto the Klein ranch in Sparta early Sunday morning, long before the sun would rise. The rolling hills were covered with trucks, cars and campers. For the three-day event contestants and the public alike shared the rustic campgrounds. The atmosphere was partylike, a lot of beer being drunk and music played. And every night the rodeo held a big dance: cowboys, cowgirls, campers and public all invited. But by this hour everything was quiet.

Parking her truck, Dana gave Windrunner a quick check, backed him out of the trailer, tied him to the side, filled his water bucket and gave him some hay. Then, wearily, she crawled into the back of her truck and fell promptly to sleep.

Raindrops hitting the top of the cab woke her. For a moment the staccato left her confused, then she remembered where she was and why. Slipping on a plastic rain jacket, she hurried to put Windrunner into the trailer, where he'd stay dry, then ran for an outhouse.

Later, at the concession stand, Dana was waiting for a cup of hot coffee when Sharon came waddling up. "My god, what I'd give for one decent john," she lamented, inching under the overhang to keep out of the rain. "Can you believe these Porta Potti's? And me having to go every ten minutes. I swear Junior's sitting on my bladder."

Dana laughed, but knew what Sharon was going through. She remembered her mother complaining of exactly the same problem the month before Danny was born. "You've dropped," she told her friend, noticing how much lower she was carrying the baby.

"You're telling me? A coffee, a milk and four sweet rolls," Sharon ordered.

"Doesn't it worry you, being up here, so far away from home? What if the baby comes?"

Sharon rubbed the front of her slicker. "Then the baby comes. If Cody wins here, he'll have the regional championship for both steer wrestling and bronc riding all sewn up. It'll be party time."

"And you didn't want to miss the party." She knew Sharon. The woman loved parties. "You're not going to make it to the end of the month."

"I sure hope not."

Dana chuckled at her friend's wholehearted response.

Sharon stared at Dana's face for a second, then shook her head. "You know, you look as bad as Garth does. You two need to get more sleep."

"I haven't seen Garth in two weeks," Dana confessed. She also hadn't seen her friend for that long.

"You haven't?" Sharon's green eyes widened with surprise. "Well, I just said 'hi' to him. He's over at your truck."

9

"GARTH'S HERE?" Dana choked on the coffee she was drinking.

Sharon grinned. "Well, it sure looked and sounded like him. You haven't heard from him in two weeks? What happened?"

"I'll tell you later," called Dana, tossing out the rest of her coffee and running for her truck.

Garth was sitting in his Bronco when she saw him. He was parked right next to her truck and was looking her way. His door opened before she reached the trailer and he stepped out, smiling. "I got your message."

Even covered with a clear plastic raincoat, he looked good. His blue-and-white striped oxford-cloth shirt was open at the neck, the sleeves rolled up to his elbows, and his stone-washed jeans fit his legs perfectly. She did notice that his tennis shoes were already soaked and covered with mud, and droplets of water clung to his hair. Someday he'd learn that boots were a better choice of footwear when attending a rodeo and that a Western hat kept both sun and rain off the head and face, but at the moment she didn't care what he did or didn't wear. He was here. That was all that mattered.

When she stopped running, her breathing was a little uneven, but she wasn't sure if it was from the exertion or just from seeing Garth. With a smile that matched his, she walked straight into his open arms. Their rainwear scrunched and crackled as it rubbed together.

"I've missed you." Dana sighed in contentment. His embrace was heaven and his strength was what she'd longed for.

"Not half as much as I've missed you." He took off her hat and kissed her forehead, then her eyelids, her cheeks and finally her mouth.

His lips met with hers in an eager reunion, and they ignored the rain falling on their heads and streaming down their faces. Tongues touched, tasted and teased, while hands held and hugged. Two weeks of misery were being released. Feeling the curves of her body, Garth remembered the marvelous ways Dana knew to please him. His body responded and he lifted his head, looking around.

Private was not the word to describe their surroundings, yet Garth wanted to make love to her. "Shall we check out the back of your truck?"

She laughed, feeling happier than she'd been in days— weeks. "We should have bought the If It's Rocking, Don't Come Knocking sign we saw at that fair in Illinois."

"If anyone knocks, we'll tell them we're not home." Again he kissed her forehead. She tasted so sweet. "Oh, Dana, I'm so glad you called. If you hadn't, I would have. I've thought about you constantly—missed you."

She pushed herself back so that she could look at him. "Sure, and that's why you forced yourself to go out. Right?"

He looked confused.

"I called you at least a hundred times Thursday night, then again Friday morning. You weren't sitting around pining for me."

Understanding, he smiled and drew her back into his embrace. "A hundred times, eh. And left only one message?"

"I hate those machines." Dana noticed he hadn't said where he'd been. She didn't like the feeling, but she was jealous.

He considered letting her go on thinking he had been out, then decided he didn't want any lies between them. "I was in Detroit. Thursday afternoon, all day Friday and Saturday morning. I was meeting with some dealers and manufacturers. And—since I was there—I went to a couple of Tigers games—and not with a woman. How could I, when she would only have reminded me of you?"

In his arms Dana felt more secure than she had Thursday night. "You could have, you know. I have no claim on you."

"Oh, yes, you do." His lips brushed over a rain-wet cheek. "I would have joined you last night, but I didn't get back to Kalamazoo until Saturday afternoon. Then I went straight to the store. I didn't get your message until late."

"See! What good are those machines if you don't get the messages?" she teased.

"I'm here, aren't I?"

"Yes, you are." Content, she nuzzled his neck.

"And we're getting soaked."

"Yes, we are. Maybe we had better crawl into my truck."

Garth noticed other campers were up, scurrying toward the outhouses, water faucets and concession stand. It was a regular highway past Dana's truck. He wanted her, but he didn't particularly relish the idea of their coming-together entertaining an entire campground. "Maybe we'd better wait on that. Have you had breakfast yet?"

"A cup of coffee." Suddenly she was starving.

"I thought you didn't drink coffee."

"I thought I'd give it a try. Something hot sounded good this morning, and coffee was all they had at the concession stand. But it didn't taste any good."

"Then let's go into town and get you some hot breakfast. While we eat, we can talk."

Dana held back. "First, I have to take care of Windrunner."

As soon as the words were out, she wondered what Garth's reaction would be. Once again she'd put her horse first. She didn't want it that way, but she didn't know what else to do. The gelding did have needs that had to be met.

But Garth merely nodded. "Can I help?"

Relieved, Dana accepted his offer. "You can get his water."

WITH WINDRUNNER taken care of, they drove into Sparta and found a coffee shop. For the first time in two weeks, Dana ate with enthusiasm. Everything tasted great—the pancakes, eggs, bacon and sausage. She even finished the toast and orange slice Garth pushed aside. Watching her, he shook his head. "When was the last time you had a decent meal?"

"I don't remember," she answered truthfully.

In his arms, she'd felt thinner than he remembered. And now that she had her raincoat off, she looked thinner. It seemed she'd suffered from their separation as much as he had. Perversely, he was glad. He'd had a miserable two weeks away from her. He hated to admit it, but he'd fallen in love. It wasn't sensible or convenient, but it had happened.

The first week after leaving Dana, he'd tried to deny it. He'd even called an old friend and asked her out, thinking a night on the town would help him forget. But he never went through with the date. An hour before he was to pick her up, he'd called and canceled.

Once he realized he loved Dana, his problem was deciding what to do about it. He'd been tired the night they argued and shouldn't have said some of the things he had. But one thing was true: he didn't want to be second in her life.

Staring at her, watching her nibble the orange sections away from the peel, he knew he would have come here even if she hadn't called. He'd thought going to Detroit might help get his mind off her, but it hadn't. Even watching the Tigers play, he'd missed her. He'd decided he had to see her and had planned on calling her folks to find out where she was. Hearing her voice on his answering machine had been a miracle, like finding a classic in perfect condition at a bargain price.

"So how're your stepfather and mother?" Dana asked, finally pushing her plate away.

Garth put down his coffee cup. "Ben's doing better all the time. He's home now and Mom says the doctors feel he'll be back to normal in six months. How are your folks? I talked to your mother. She's the one who told me where I'd find you. But I forgot to ask how things were going." He'd been too eager to see Dana again to think of anything else.

"Dad's getting worried about the mortgage—and so am I. Between what I've earned with the barrel racing and what he's made off calves, we have a little more than five thousand dollars saved up. He'll sell the rest of the calves this month, but we'll be a long way from twenty thousand." She looked out the restaurant window. Water was streaming down the glass in sheets. In the past hour, at least an inch of rain had fallen.

Garth followed her gaze. "If it doesn't stop, what will you do?"

"I don't know."

"Will they delay the rodeo?"

"I don't know." She looked back at him. "If they don't, I'll just have to do my best."

"It doesn't seem fair." The weather the day before had been beautiful—sunny and warm. Overnight the clouds had covered the sky and the temperature had dropped twenty degrees. "Those who ran yesterday had better conditions."

"It's the chance we each take. I could have asked for Saturday. I didn't."

"Dana, if it's raining like this, please don't run."

He said it softly, and the gentle plea in his eyes tore at her heart. She looked away, her answer not much more than a whisper. "I have to."

"I'll sell the Thunderbird. I know I can get twenty thousand for it. That will take care of the mortgage." It was a spur-of-the-moment decision, but it sounded good. Dana's safety was far more important than a car.

Surprised, her eyes met with his again. "You'd sell the T-Bird? For me?"

Reaching across the table, he took her hand. "Honey, I love you. I don't want you hurt."

Dana went perfectly still. *He loves you*, her mind repeated. *No!* she wanted to cry out, but didn't. Taking a deep breath, she closed her eyes.

Garth could feel the tension in her fingers and knew his words hadn't had the effect he'd hoped they would. He'd tried to consider the possibility that she might not feel the same way, but her call had made him forget everything. "Dana, I'm not asking for any kind of commitment from you. It's just how I feel. I can't help it."

Her lashes rose slowly, and she again looked at him. She should be thrilled that this man loved her; instead she was scared. "I don't know how I feel," she admitted truthfully. She wanted him—physically and emotionally—but love?

That meant commitment, marriage. Forever after. Damn John, he'd made her so wary.

"Then that's what I'll have to accept for now," he said quietly. He had no choice. His time away from her had proven that.

She sighed, squeezed his fingers, then remembered what they'd been talking about. "But I won't let you sell your car."

"And why not?"

"Because it's too much to ask." She knew how much he loved that old car. She'd ridden in it to lunch a few times, and he'd taken it the night they'd had dinner and gone to the play. While they were at his apartment, he'd shown her step-by-step pictures and told her about the hours the restoration had taken and the problems he'd had finding the parts. To Garth, the Thunderbird wasn't just a vehicle, it was his baby, to be coddled and adored.

"You're not asking, I'm offering."

"Garth, I don't want you to."

"And what if I sell it anyway?"

"Then that's your decision, but I won't take the money." Her grip on his hand tightened. "Please, don't. I'd always feel guilty if you did."

"Dana, don't you see, *I* feel guilty. I want to help your family. I like them and don't want to see them lose the farm any more than you do. But my money's all tied up with the new store. My car's the only thing I can offer."

"I know . . . and I do understand." She wished she could make *him* understand. "But I just can't let you do it. This is my problem. I had it before we even met. You've helped a lot as it is. Who knows, maybe I'll luck out today. Maybe the rain will stop."

"And maybe it won't."

By ONE-THIRTY, the rain had diminished to a light drizzle and the arena was disked and dragged so there were no standing puddles and the ground was as safe as possible. In the Grand Entry Dana wore her rain jacket over her green outfit and tipped her hat to the hardy souls who had ventured out to watch. On the hill that overlooked the arena and under the trees that edged it, the audience sat on blankets and oilcloths, on lawn chairs and coolers, and drank coffee, soft drinks and beer while trying to keep the rain off with umbrellas and plastic. And, as long as there was an audience, the show would go on.

From breakfast until it was time to saddle up, Garth had tried to talk Dana out of participating. He'd appealed to her emotionally and mentally, telling her she was endangering her life and her horse's. But she'd argued that she was too close to quit, that she didn't have to come in first—she just had to place and beat Connie—and that the girl would be running under the same conditions. Finally he'd stopped badgering her and helped her get ready.

The bareback bronc riding came right after the opening ceremonies. With Windrunner tied to the trailer, Dana and Garth joined Sharon at the fence to watch Cody. "He drew a good rank horse," Sharon said. "Now, if he can just get a good score."

Suddenly Sharon grimaced and clenched her fingers around the railing.

"You all right?" Dana was worried. Sharon had gone pale, her jaw rigid.

Sharon nodded and slowly relaxed. At last she smiled. "Just a twinge. Junior letting me know he's around."

"Shouldn't you be sitting down?" asked Garth, also concerned by what he'd seen.

"Maybe." Sharon looked down at the wet grass at her feet. "We've got some lawn chairs back at the truck. I wish I'd brought one over."

Garth dropped his plastic raincoat on the grass. "You sit on this for now, while I go get your chair. Where's your truck parked?"

Sharon gave him directions, and he was off. Ten minutes later he was back, lawn chair in hand. Opening it, he made certain it was level, then helped Sharon to her feet and into the chair.

Sharon bowed her head in appreciation, sighing in relief. "Dana, you've got yourself a gentleman. Better hang on to him."

"I'll try." Taking Garth's hand in hers, Dana gave his fingers a squeeze. She wanted to hang on, but they still had so many problems to resolve.

Nine cowboys were competing in the bareback event; Cody was scheduled last, on a bronc called This One's For You. Bucking, slipping and sliding, one by one, eight horses came out of the chutes—one nearly climbing out before the door opened. Each rider whooped and spurred, trying to influence the two judges into giving them high scores. Mud flew, spattering horses, riders and those standing nearby. Four cowboys failed to make the horn and covered with mud from head to toe, limped out of the arena. One was disqualified by the mark-out rule, his feet going behind the horse's shoulder, while the three who did make it for six seconds had scores in the high seventies.

Sharon, Garth and Dana all held their breaths when chute number nine opened. Cody's horse went straight up, then landed with a jar, mud splashing around his hooves. Head down, he crow-hopped and sunfished. As usual, Dana counted off the seconds with her fingers crossed. Her other hand was being squeezed by Garth's fingers, and she knew he was as intensely involved as any of them.

And when Cody made it to the horn, three audible sighs told their concern. Then they laughed. But it wasn't until the pickup rider had Cody safely off the still-bucking bronc that Sharon's expression truly relaxed. And when the announcer gave Cody's score, Sharon leaned back in her chair and patted her stomach. "Daddy did it, Junior. If anyone beats that score, I'll be surprised."

They stayed and watched Cody in the steer-wrestling event. "He's thinkin' of buying a horse," Sharon told them. "He's getting tired of paying out a quarter of his winnings every time he borrows a cowboy's horse. He says he's gonna get a good horse and let a few cowboys pay him for a change."

Cody's time was good enough for a second place if no one beat it Monday. After Cody left the arena, Dana headed back to her truck. She was too nervous to watch any more. Garth followed her.

"No changing your mind?" he asked, resting a hand on her shoulder.

"No changing my mind." She had to do it. Turning, she faced him. "Garth, don't worry. I promise I won't take any chances. Windrunner's not a motorcycle. There's no concrete wall out there. I'm not going to get hurt."

He stared into her dark eyes and wished he felt as optimistic as she sounded. He knew she would take chances. She had to; it was part of the game. And he knew she could get hurt. That was also a part of the game. He couldn't stop her. There was really only one thing he could do. Drawing her close, he kissed her.

His demanding mouth expressed his need for her, and Dana responded with an equal need. Silently she promised that as soon as her event was over, she and Garth would leave. She'd take Windrunner home, then go with him. They needed time together, time to talk—time to make love. Her place, his apartment—it didn't matter where. She'd forget the rodeo she was supposed to go to tomorrow, pay the penalty, gladly. She was through putting Garth second.

"Good luck," he murmured when he finally let her go.

WINDRUNNER SEEMED to know his turn was next. Through her legs and the reins, Dana could feel the horse's tension. Only her steady pressure on the bit kept him from taking off. He couldn't stand still: his legs moving constantly, he shifted his weight from side to side.

With her hands and voice she tried to calm him. He needed to expend his energy inside the arena, not here outside the gate. The sheen of sweat on his shoulders was not a good sign.

Dana's eyes darted to the railing. Garth was there, watching her. She could tell by the taut line of his mouth and the way he kept running his fingers through his hair that he was worried. In a minute it would be over—then all three of them could relax.

Everyone was running slow. They'd been running slow the day before. Seventeen point nine two three seconds was the time to beat. She was sure she could do it; at least she was going to give it her best try.

The gate opened and a mud-spattered cowgirl and her equally mud-spattered horse loped out. "Eighteen point five seventy-two," called the announcer. "Next is a gal who's running neck and neck with teenager Connie Birch for the regional championship. This is called a turna-round rodeo. A win here can move a rider from second to world champion. Miss Dana Allen."

Dana barely heard the applause. Windrunner was high. He bounded through the gate and into the arena. She pulled him down to a lope and forced him to make a circle. With every step he tried to break free from her hold on his mouth, but she wanted to feel the ground before tripping the timer. Her arms ached as she straightened him out. The turf was wet, but better than she'd expected. Her horse should be able to handle it. Squeezing with her legs, her eyes on the first barrel, she let Windrunner go.

True to his name, he ran like the wind. Dana's hat was blown back, so that the cold air whipped her bangs and the drizzle hit her face. A spray of mud spewed out behind her horse's flying hooves.

The first barrel was reached, circled and left; the second was coming up fast. Dana willed Windrunner not to overrun it, and he obeyed, making a good, tight turn. Now only the third barrel remained.

It worried her the most. She'd seen two horses slip going around that barrel. The footing had to be bad there. A thousand pounds of horse running full out, suddenly slowing and turning, could easily fall. But a fast, tight turn was what she needed.

Take it easy. She could almost hear Garth's voice in her head. *It's not worth getting hurt for.*

But she couldn't take it easy—not if she wanted to win. Her time so far was good. She could feel it—knew it from having made so many runs. In spite of the rain and the mud and the cold, she could win today. "Win, win, win," she chanted, swinging her weight into the barrel.

They were almost around it when Dana felt Windrunner's haunches dip. The ground was too slick, his speed too fast. The mud-brown dirt was giving beneath his hind legs, his entire body slanting toward the barrel. In her mind she remembered a similar feeling, just a little over a year before. Her horse was going down.

Holding on to the horn, Dana swung her weight to the right, trying to help her horse regain his balance. He lurched forward, wobbled, then found his footing. Another stride and Windrunner was around the barrel, running for the finish.

Yet something didn't feel quite right. His stride wasn't smooth, his rhythm was off. She didn't use the bat clenched in her teeth to ask for more speed. Only with her hands and legs did she urge him on. Over the line she passed, then quickly she pulled him down. Windrunner immediately slowed, and at a controlled lope they left the arena.

Dana was off as soon as they cleared the entryway. She knew she had a problem.

"And the time for that run..." the announcer said. "The time..."

Dana walked Windrunner a few feet. He was definitely limping, favoring his right hind leg.

"It seems the timer didn't work, folks. Mud was thrown onto the lens when the horse crossed the line. However, Miss Allen will have a chance to go again. Next is..."

Garth was running her way.

She kept her eyes on her horse, walking him. He was now barely putting any weight on that leg. Bringing him to a stop, she first checked his hoof for a stone. There was none.

Garth stopped beside her. "What's he mean you'll have to go again? It's not your fault the timer didn't work. Why didn't they have a backup?"

"Because they didn't, I guess. It's called luck, and mine seems to have turned bad." She was moving her hand up

Windrunner's leg, feeling for heat. When she flexed his hock, the horse pulled away. "Damn!"

"What is it?" asked Garth, not quite sure what she was doing or why.

Tears of frustration and disappointment formed in her eyes. It wasn't fair—just wasn't fair. Chewing on her lower lip, she looked at Garth. He'd been right. She'd taken a chance, pushed for the faster, not the safer way. But she wasn't the one hurt. It was her horse. "I think he pulled a tendon when he slipped going around that last barrel."

"How serious is that?"

"I don't know. Maybe I'm wrong. Maybe it's just a strain he can walk off."

She looked back at the gate she'd just left. *No time. No money.* She had nothing. Connie would still be ahead. If she'd just placed, she might have cinched the championship. If only. . .

Again she looked at her horse. If she used a painkiller, she could run him again. She had some in the truck for emergencies. Given one now, in a few minutes Windrunner wouldn't know his leg hurt.

The horse took a halting step, and Dana cleared her mind of such thoughts. She would not do that to her horse—to any horse. She might give Windrunner the medication, but it would be to ease his pain, not to run him into the ground. "Garth, tell them I won't be going in again."

"It's that bad?"

"It's that bad."

While he delivered her message, Dana led Windrunner back to the trailer. The horse wasn't showing any signs of walking off this injury. With each step, he seemed to be getting worse.

"What happened?" Charlene Harmond yelled as Windrunner limped passed her truck.

Charlene was an old-timer on the circuit and an officer of the Great Lakes Barrel Racing Association. She'd had some good years in the past, but was riding a new horse this summer and having more problems than successes. Although Dana wouldn't call Charlene a close friend, she liked the woman.

"He slipped and hurt his leg," she called back.

"Need an ice pack?"

Dana paused and felt Windrunner's hock. It was definitely hot and swelling. "Have you got one?"

"Give me a second to find it. I'll bring it over to your trailer."

Garth found Charlene and Dana kneeling behind Windrunner, working on the horse's leg. He'd vented his anger on a few people but wasn't satisfied with the results. He'd seen the tears in Dana's eyes and knew the emotional pain she was suffering. It was bad enough that her horse was hurt, but to have run as well as she had and have the timer malfunction was ridiculous. And he'd told them so. In no uncertain terms.

Not that it did him any good. Apologies wouldn't win her the money or points she needed.

"What'd they say?" Dana asked when she saw him.

"That they were sorry, but there was nothing they could do about it. I told them they could give you the points."

Charlene looked up from the bandage she was using to keep the ice pack in place. "And I'm sure they agreed to that."

Garth grunted. "How's his leg?"

"I won't know for a while." She'd wanted a romantic night with Garth. Now it looked as if she'd be spending the night sitting up with her horse.

"Dana?"

It wasn't Charlene calling her name. Or Garth. The quavering summons came from behind, and Dana turned to see Sharon—her face as pale as her hair and her green eyes wide with fear. She was leaning heavily against the fender of the old Ford, and even though it was still cool out, a sheen of perspiration covered her skin, and her maternity jeans were soaked on the inside thighs.

"Sharon, what's wrong?" cried Dana, immediately rising to her feet.

"My—my water broke. The baby's coming."

10

GARTH MOVED as quickly as Dana did and they reached
Sharon's side simultaneously. He wasn't exactly sure what
to do, but he could see that the woman was close to col-
lapsing and he slid an arm around her for support.
"Where's Cody?"

"Gone to look at a horse." Sharon glanced up at Garth,
then looked at Dana. "I don't know what to do."

"Don't worry, we'll take care of you," said Dana, and
Garth nodded in agreement. "How far apart are the contractions?" She hoped she wouldn't be playing midwife.
It was one thing to help her father with the cows—another to deliver a baby.

"I'm not sure. Five, six minutes . . . I think."

Sharon clenched her teeth and leaned forward, putting
her hands on her abdomen, and Dana knew a contraction
was starting then. "Three-thirty," she said, glancing at her
watch, then she touched Sharon's arm. Having gone with
her mother to a couple of birthing classes before her
brother was born, Dana knew it would be easier on Sharon if she was relaxed. "Don't fight it. Breathe with it. Try
to relax. Do you want to sit down? Lie down?"

Sharon shook her head, panting.

"Shouldn't we get her to a hospital?" The pallor of the
woman's skin worried Garth.

"She doesn't look good," reflected Charlene, having
joined them.

"Sharon, when will Cody be back?" Dana asked. She'd like to kick the cowboy's butt for choosing this time to look at a horse.

"He said he wouldn't be long." Sharon kept panting, leaning against Garth. "The guy doesn't live far from here.... He talked to Cody before the show.... Since he was done...Cody decided to give the horse a quick look."

Dana knew how those "quick looks" went. Put two horsemen together and they could talk for hours. Sharon's situation wouldn't wait for his return. She looked at Charlene. "Where's the nearest hospital?"

"Your best bet is to take her to Grand Rapids. You want me to take Windrunner home with me? I was planning on leavin' soon. And if you'd like, I can call my vet and have him look at the leg. You could pick him up whenever you wanted."

That would certainly eliminate one problem. And she trusted Charlene. The woman would see to it that Windrunner received immediate attention and good care. Not only that, she lived just a half hour south of Sparta; this way, Windrunner would be in a stall and tended to a lot sooner than if they drove him back to the farm. It was an easy decision. "Thanks, Char. I owe you one."

"No problem. I'll catch you another time. Also, if Cody doesn't get back before I go, I'll spread the word and leave a note on his truck." She chuckled. "I'll tell him he'd better hustle or he's gonna miss the arrival of next year's rookie." Charlene leaned forward and squeezed Sharon's arm. "Take it easy, kid."

Sharon nodded, her breathing not yet even, but the contraction was obviously easing.

"We'll take the Bronco," said Garth, knowing the back seat was already down and Sharon could stretch out.

"I'm sorry for having to bother you," Sharon apologized. She straightened and took a step toward Garth's car. "I wish Cody were here."

"So do we," agreed Dana, hurrying to get ahead to open the back while Garth continued to keep his arm around Sharon's shoulders for support. "But since he's not, we get to accompany you to the grand entry."

They helped ease Sharon in, and Dana climbed in the back with her. If the baby did decide to come en route, she wanted to be where she could help. As Garth drove off, she waved at Charlene and crossed her fingers. She was wishing for two things now: that Windrunner's leg would be all right and that they'd make it to the hospital in time.

Before leaving the campgrounds, Garth got directions to the hospital. Two turns and they were on Highway 37, heading south. When Sharon started another contraction, Dana glanced at her watch. Three thirty-seven. Seven minutes had passed since the start of the last one. They should make it. The first child usually took a while to arrive. The problem with babies, though, was you never knew. Sharon could easily move into the final stages of labor within minutes. "Better hustle," she called forward to Garth.

He did exactly as she instructed. Pressing down on the gas pedal, he reverted to his racing days. The Bronco became a streak of tan—a four-wheel-drive ambulance zipping around cars, honking to get others to move over. Any and all speed limits were ignored.

Dana held her breath when they passed through a business section and Garth didn't slow at a yellow light. Then he hung a tight right to get onto Highway 96, scooting both Dana and Sharon to the side, and she called out. "Whoa! Slow down. We want to get her there in one piece."

"Too rough back there?" He'd been so intent on getting to the hospital as fast as possible, he'd forgotten the back of the Bronco didn't ride as smoothly as the front. Immediately he did slow down.

"And I accused you of being afraid to go fast?" Dana laughed at the idea.

"I'm scared," Sharon confessed, gripping Dana's hand. "What if Cody doesn't make it in time? What if *we* don't make it in time?" Another contraction was beginning and she gritted her teeth as she spoke, tears streaming down her cheeks. "What if something's wrong with the baby? I'm too early."

Dana didn't bother to check her watch. The time between contractions wasn't as important as Sharon's peace of mind. Assuming as casual an attitude as she could muster, she tried to get Sharon to relax. "Nothing's going to be wrong with your baby. Junior's just decided he's tired of hearing you talk about rodeos. He wanted to see this one for himself. He'll probably come out of the chute kickin' and hollerin', just like his daddy always does."

"Probably," Sharon agreed, panting. "Will you stay with me until Cody comes?"

"I'll stay with you until Cody and Junior both arrive," Dana promised. "You couldn't get me to leave."

At the hospital a nurse took charge of Sharon, Garth parked the car and Dana gave the admittance clerk as much information as she could supply on Sharon and Cody. A half hour later, she and Garth were pacing back and forth in the waiting room when a young, pretty, redheaded nurse came in and called Dana's name.

"Here," said Dana, turning to face the woman.

"Your friend's been prepped. She's not fully dilated so it's going to be a while before the baby comes. Any way to get hold of her husband?"

"We have no idea where he is, but as soon as he gets back to the rodeo grounds, they'll send him here." She'd bet by now every cowboy and cowgirl in Sparta knew about Sharon's condition. Cody would be told as soon as he returned.

"If you two would like, you can go in with her now."

The room they were escorted to was cozy and cheerful, one of the new family rooms that were intended to make having a baby a more natural event. Sharon lay on the bed, her head propped up on a pillow. Garth and Dana sat down beside her.

"Junior's ready, but I'm not." Sharon sighed. She wasn't as pale, but she looked tired.

"You know what's ahead—all the dirty diapers, formula to fix, bottles to wash. You're not as eager to get into this motherhood act as Junior is ready to be a baby," Dana teased.

Sharon didn't smile. "I wish Cody was here."

"He'll be comin' soon." Dana tried to keep Sharon talking. They discussed the horse Cody was looking at and might buy, talked about the cradle he'd made for the baby and both complained about the cost of paint, Sharon describing the soft shade of blue she'd used in the nursery. And, during contractions, Dana helped Sharon relax and breathe.

Garth said little, but he was a help. It was reassuring to Dana just to have him by her side. And when the nurse sent them out into the hallway while the doctor examined Sharon, she welcomed the warmth and support of Garth's arms.

"This isn't how I'd planned spending this evening," she murmured, pressing her cheek against his shoulder and listening to the steady beat of his heart.

"Oh, and how did you plan on spending this evening?" his low, husky voice whispered into her ear.

"With you. Maybe at my place . . . maybe at yours."

"Hmm." He bent his head down and nibbled on her earlobe. "Sounds good to me."

"To talk." As he attacked her ear, she wiggled her hips against his.

"Yes, to talk." He half groaned, the feel of her body arousing many good feelings.

"To work out some problems."

"Hmm. I definitely have a problem we could work on." His tongue dipped seductively into the hollow of her ear, then out.

"And I'm sure we both need some rest."

"In bed." His breathing was growing ragged. With most women, he had a great deal of control; with Dana, he seemed to have none. His lips traveled over her cheek and neck.

His face was rough with a day's growth of beard, but Dana didn't mind. And when his lips touched hers, she felt as if she'd come home. She'd missed his kisses, his gentle power.

"Ahhem."

At the sound of a man clearing his throat, Dana and Garth abruptly broke apart and turned to face the middle-aged doctor who had been examining Sharon.

"Better watch out. That's what leads to a reservation in one of these rooms." Smiling, the doctor nodded toward the labor room.

Dana felt her cheeks glow. Garth simply grinned and possessively slipped his arm back around her shoulders.

"I thought I'd better give you a progress report," the doctor continued, turning professional. "Your friend's doing well. She's almost fully dilated, and it won't be long before we're ready to deliver the baby. Any idea when the father might arrive?"

"Your guess is as good as ours," said Dana. *Soon*, she prayed. *Very soon*.

As if in answer to her prayers, a deep, gravelly voice traveled around the corner and down the hallway. "Where's my wife?"

Dana grinned and Garth squeezed her shoulders.

Cody Wright looked ready to take on a herd of wild horses when he rounded the corner. Cowboy hat on his head, the spurs on his boots clinking with each step, he strode toward them. His expression of concern turned to relief when he saw them, then back to concern. "Am I too late? Has she had the baby? Is Sharon all right?"

"She's all right, but it's a good thing you got here when you did," Dana answered. Turning to the doctor, she made the necessary introductions.

In a second the doctor and Cody were back in with Sharon, and Garth and Dana were again alone. The need for them to be at the hospital was over, but Dana didn't want to leave. "Do you mind staying . . . at least until she has the baby?"

"You couldn't get me to go." Garth chuckled. "I want to see if Junior comes out a miniature version of Cody."

Restless, they wandered the hall, then visited the nursery. Tiny bassinets held tiny babies bundled in cotton blankets. Standing at the window, Garth and Dana looked in. "Do you like children?" he asked.

"Oh, yes." Dana watched a nurse pick up one infant. "Babies are always so cute and cuddly. When Danny was born, I loved helping Mom feed and bathe him. Can't say I was wild about changing his diapers, though." She smiled, remembering her first experience and how she'd tried to change the diaper without looking or breathing.

The nurse was doing a much more efficient job. "What about you? Do you like children?"

"I like them, but—"

"But what?" she asked when he didn't go on.

His brow furrowed with concern, Garth looked her way, shrugged, then looked back at the babies. "But sometimes I worry about having children . . . about what kind of father I might be. I don't want to be like my dad."

Taking his hand in hers, Dana turned to face him. "I don't think you would be, Garth."

"I walked out on you two weeks ago," he reminded her.

"With good reason. I wasn't being fair to you. I *was* putting you second. I've been so wrapped up with getting the money, I really haven't thought of much else. Now, with Win hurt . . ." She couldn't finish.

"Dana, don't give up," Garth urged.

They heard Cody in the hallway, his voice booming as he asked a nurse where they were. Garth and Dana stepped away from the window and out into the hallway so Cody could see them.

"Has Junior arrived?" asked Dana. "Have him signed up for tomorrow's bronc ride, yet?"

"Junior had a surprise for us." Cody laughed, tears of pride still shining in his eyes. "More'n likely she'll want to chase those barrels than ride broncs."

"A girl?" Sharon had been so sure the baby would be a boy, Dana had assumed she'd be right.

"Seven pounds three ounces and already vocally asserting herself."

"What did you name her?" asked Dana. She knew a boy would have been named after Cody. She'd simply never thought to ask Sharon what they would name a girl.

"Tammye Sharie Wright." Proudly, Cody spelled the name out for them. "They're bringin' her down here to the nursery to check her out. As soon as Sharon's in her room, the doctor said you all can go in and see her."

He was so excited, he could hardly stand still. "Know where a pay phone is? I gotta make some calls. There's a pair of grandmas and grandpas who'll want to know about this."

"The waiting room has one," Garth said.

Cody left to make his calls, and seconds later Garth and Dana had a chance to see the new baby. Tammye Sharie wasn't overjoyed with her surroundings; her little fists were clenched, her eyes closed tight and her face beet-red as she screamed her protests. They watched the nurses care for her, and the baby had stopped crying by the time they walked away from the window.

After Cody finished his calls, Dana called Charlene to tell her about the baby and check up on Windrunner. Garth, meanwhile, offered to go to the gift shop and find something appropriate for a baby girl. Ten minutes later Dana joined him.

"What do you think of this?" he asked, holding up a king-size teddy bear. "Or this?" He wound up a carousel music box and set it down to play.

Dana considered the two gifts.

Garth reached out to touch a wisp of hair that had pulled loose from her scarf and dangled near her cheek. "You talked to Charlene?"

"Yes."

He brushed his fingertips over the strand, feeling its fine texture, then slipped it behind her ear. "How's Windrunner?"

"Comfortable, she said. Her vet's been to see him and he said the best thing to do was rest him up for a few days, then, if the leg's not better, have it X-rayed." Dana glanced up at Garth. "I told her I'd pick him up tomorrow some-time."

"Tomorrow?" His eyebrows rose. He'd expected her to insist on getting the horse back to the farm as soon as possible.

"I see no reason to rush home tonight. The vet gave Win something for pain so he's comfortable, and Char said she'd keep an eye on him. I thought maybe we could find a motel and stay over. When they say those campgrounds at Sparta are rustic, they mean rustic. I can't tell you how much I'd love a hot shower."

He smiled, happier than she could ever imagine. He knew she had to be worried about her horse, yet she was making time for them. "One hot shower coming up."

They chose the music box and took it to Sharon's room. The baby was brought in while they talked. Tammye Sharie was now more content, her skin less red, and tiny wisps of blond hair showed on the top of her head. Proudly Cody showed off his new daughter.

An hour later Dana and Garth left the hospital. One quick stop at a motel reserved a room, then they returned to the rodeo grounds.

Dana was glad she didn't have a long drive ahead of her. They'd pick up her truck and trailer, then she'd follow Garth back to the motel. Within an hour they should be settled in. It would be an evening to relax. Glancing over at Garth, she smiled. Actually, an evening of relaxation wasn't exactly what she had in mind.

IT TOOK LONGER to get to the motel than Dana had anticipated, primarily because every cowgirl and cowboy they ran into wanted a detailed report on Sharon, Cody and the new baby. Finally they were able to break away. The drive back to Grand Rapids was slower and safer than the one they'd taken earlier that day, and it was nearly dark when Dana parked her pickup and empty horse trailer at the back of the motel. Garth pulled his Bronco up next to her. Quickly she got her tote bag and a change of clothes out of the back of the truck and locked up, then turned to find herself wedged between Garth's solid body and her tailgate. "Want to use the shower in my room?" he asked seductively.

She remembered the similar scenario they'd played in only a few weeks before. How much had happened since then. Batting her lashes, her dark eyes dancing with delight, she asked, "Do you have a hair dryer?"

"Oh, I'm sure I can find a way to dry your hair." He bent close and blew into her hair. Then his mouth covered hers and his arms went around her.

For endless seconds they were lost in a kiss. The worries and excitement of the day were forgotten as each found pleasure in the taste and feel of the other. Then, slowly, they remembered where they were and that what they were doing could be better done behind a closed door. Wordlessly they pulled apart, staring into each other's eyes, then suddenly they both began to laugh. Locking arms, they headed for their room.

Bouncing on the king-size bed, testing its hardness, Dana glanced around the small room. A bed, a dresser, a table, a chair, a television and a nightstand. Nothing fancy, but it would do. The mattress was firm and the bathroom spacious. "First dibs," she called.

"On what?" Garth set his bag down next to her tote on the dresser. In the mirror he could see her. She looked like a kid bouncing on the bed. And he felt like a kid—on his first date. Tonight would be special.

"On the shower." Pulling the scarf from her hair, she ran her fingers through snarled tresses. "I'm a mess."

"A cute mess." Turning, he faced her. "I'll wash your back."

Grinning, she let her eyes run the length of him. "And I'll wash your front."

"It's a deal."

He gave her a few minutes of privacy in the bathroom, waiting until he heard the shower turn on before opening the door. Her mud-spattered clothes were in a pile, her boots to the side. She'd already stepped under the water, and he began to undress.

"A country-grow'd woman—" she began to sing "—and a city-bred man."

He shook his head and unbuttoned his shirt. Whatever the tune was supposed to be, she was fracturing it.

"Met alongside the highway, one fateful night."

Off went the shirt, then his shoes.

"Oh, country and city, they're two worlds apart. But—" She faltered, not quite sure what she wanted to say next.

He dropped his pants by hers and stepped toward the shower. "Country and city—" he sang, imitating her country twang "—will git along fine."

Dana watched as he pulled back the curtain. He was gorgeous, his body lean and sinewy—all male—and partially aroused. He wanted her, and she wanted him.

"Stop worrying about our differences," Garth soothed, stepping into the tub in front of her and blocking the spray of the shower head. His eyes moved over her shimmering wet body. "I like our differences."

Visually they devoured each other, and when their gazes met again, she smiled. "So do I."

"And we're not worlds apart." Leaning forward, he touched his lips to hers. "Maybe I don't like swimming in your pond and you don't like my apartment, but we can find things in common."

Again he kissed her, and Dana slid her arms around his waist, feeling the pelting water hit the backs of her hands. She liked kissing him. They had that in common.

He drew her closer so her breasts pressed against the hairs on his muscular chest, then he touched the small of her back, bringing her hips into contact with his. He was hard and hot, and an equally fiery heat flowed through her body—a heat that had nothing to do with the warmth of the shower.

His tongue invaded her mouth, prodding and searching; his need for her was all-consuming. He'd tried to leave her but had found it impossible. Now he wanted all of her, forever. He couldn't hold her closely enough or kiss her long enough. Panting, he raised his head. "Ever done it in a shower?"

"No." Her heart was pounding, her pulse was ringing in her ears.

"Want to try?"

"Sure," she whispered, as those crazy butterflies once again took flight in her stomach. "How do we do it?"

"Just relax and I'll show you." He kissed her again—a quick peck—then reached over and grabbed the bar of soap. "But first, I promised to wash your back. Now, turn around."

She did turn around, reluctantly. She wanted him to make love to her, not scrub her down. Nevertheless he insisted, using his fingers to work each tired and strained muscle, starting at her neck and moving slowly down to her bottom. Then he squatted and the shower rinsed away the lather while Garth ran the soap over her thighs and calves.

She felt pampered and decadent, her muscles tightening when his hands moved along the insides of her thighs, teasingly close to their juncture. But he stopped short of the spot she wanted him to touch, gave her legs a little squeeze, then stood. "Now, turn around."

Her eyes met with his, and she was sure he could tell how much she wanted him—that he was driving her wild with his game—but he continued his slow, thorough application of the soap. Gently he lathered each breast, moved to the side to let the shower rinse away the suds, then leaned forward to lick away the tiny droplets of water that clung to her taut nipples. His tongue circled each nub, then he sucked one into his mouth, his lips holding it captive.

She groaned as a multitude of erotic messages were transmitted from nerve ending to nerve ending. A shudder ran the length of her and she gazed down at the top of his dark head of hair. Jolts of excitement reached the center of her, triggering deep desire. She rubbed his hair, her fingers digging in when he switched breasts and repeated his procedure. Oh, how much pleasure a man's tongue could bring! Oh, how sweet the torture of wanting, yet having to wait!

Then his hands moved lower, and his fingers traveled to the focus of her need. Touching, probing, he centered in on one spot. His lips followed the path of his hands, and Dana arched her spine and threw her head back, so that the shower sprayed against her face. Gripping his wet hair, she clung to him, letting him work his sweet magic until she could stand it no longer. Reaching the edge of control, she pushed his head back and cried, "No more. I can't take it."

He looked up, and passion-drugged eyes met with his. Slowly he rose to his feet.

"My turn," she said huskily, not sure she wanted to prolong the moment, yet wanting it to last forever. "I promised to wash your front."

"So you did," he agreed and stood, waiting.

Lathering the soap, she started with his shoulders and moved downward. The foam caught in the dark hairs that covered his chest, and she turned him to rinse it away, then leaned forward and touched a small, budding nipple with her tongue. She felt him tremble and smiled. He'd teased her; now it was her turn.

Slowly she moved one hand down his belly, rubbing the bar of soap in small circles, each stroke taking her fingers lower. Neither of them said a word, but she could feel the tension building in him and knew he was growing harder. He was barely breathing . . . waiting. His hands rested on her shoulders and when she bent down, moving her head lower, his fingers tightened slightly and he sucked in a breath.

She'd learned how to excite him, and now his enjoyment was hers; his arousal, hers. And when she was sure he could take no more, she straightened and kissed his lips. "Did you like that?"

His reply was a strangled yes, with his heart pounding in his chest. "The only thing I'd like better would be to be inside of you, to feel you around me."

"I want you inside of me," she rasped, as ready as she would ever be.

Touching her thigh, he brought her leg up until her foot rested on the edge of the tub. Water dripped over onto the linoleum, but neither noticed nor cared. His hands caressed her body, and her lips, her face. And then he positioned himself and held her close.

One hard thrust took him in, and Dana wrapped her arms around his neck, burying her face against his. Differences disappeared. They were merged together in unity. And when he moved, her body also moved, creating a rhythm of ecstasy. They were singing a new song—their song. Discord had become harmony. Her body trembled, then shook.

SLOWLY SHE GREW aware of the water hitting her arms and his back. The shower was still warm, but she'd bet they'd used half the motel's reserve of hot water. Not that it bothered her. At the moment, nothing bothered her. And considering the way Garth was nuzzling her neck, she didn't think much was bothering him.

He'd reached his climax soon after she had, his release bringing her even more pleasure. Now she could say she'd done it in the shower—not that she'd probably ever tell anyone. She grinned and looked up at his chin. "I was right the first time."

"Huh?" His gray-blue eyes held a dreamy expression.

She could tell he didn't know what she was talking about. "The first time you offered your shower. I knew it would be dangerous."

"But fun?" he questioned. He'd certainly enjoyed himself.

"Definitely fun," she agreed. There was something about a shower that made her want to sing. Right now she wanted to belt out a love song.

"Well, it's not going to be much fun if we turn into prunes." Twisting around, he pushed off the faucet and the water stopped. "I'll dry your back if you'll dry mine."

They did manage to get each other dry, but somehow the sight of the bed kept them away from their clothes. Lying on the mattress, Dana welcomed Garth. What they'd started needed to be repeated; their bodies were aching for each other. And when at last they were sated, they became a twist of arms and legs, and slept.

It was after midnight when they both woke, hungry. They took the Bronco to a fast-food restaurant and filled up on hamburgers and french fries. Laughing, they talked about Cody and Sharon and the unexpected prize those two would be taking home. Then Dana grew somber.

She'd almost forgotten what had happened in the arena that afternoon. Windrunner was hurt. And with his injury, her hopes of winning the twenty thousand dollars her folks needed for the farm were gone. No other rider in the region was close enough to take second place from her, even if she didn't ride again before the finals, but all a second place meant was that she'd be eligible to go to the International Finals Rodeo in January. Connie Birch would win the twenty thousand, the use of the truck, and the regional title.

"You were right, you know," she confessed, wishing he hadn't been.

"How's that?" He could sense the change in her mood. From a smile, she'd gone to near tears.

"I took too many chances today—yesterday. I knew the ground was wet and mushy, yet I pushed Win for all the speed I could get. I was going to win, no matter what...." She paused and sighed. "Well, I didn't. Now I've lost everything. Maybe my horse. Definitely the farm."

Garth reached over and took her hand in his. He didn't want her to cry. He didn't want her sad. Gently, reassuringly, he gave her fingers a squeeze. "Don't give up yet. If I was right once, I'm going to be right again. You're going to come out a winner."

"How?" she asked, wishing she could believe him, but not knowing any way she could. Then she remembered his earlier suggestion and shook her head. "No, Garth. I won't let you sell your car. Not for me or my folks."

He frowned. "You sure do like to make life difficult."

"Promise," she insisted.

For a minute he considered going ahead and selling it and just not telling her, then realized that would never work. She wouldn't take the money that way. Besides, their relationship had to be built on trust, not subterfuge. But darn, the woman was making it hard. He grumbled a little, then gave in. "All right, I promise I won't sell the T-Bird."

"Or the Bronco." She wasn't sure what he might try.

He looked over his shoulder, out to the parking lot. "I'm afraid that baby wouldn't bring in a third of what you need. I'd need a half-dozen Broncos around to help." He looked back at her and smiled. "Which gives me an idea."

11

GARTH WOULDN'T TELL her what his idea was. Not even later when she teased him in bed. Finally Dana gave up trying to find out. He'd have to tell her, she figured, sooner or later.

By Wednesday she still didn't know. Garth had called Monday night to make sure she'd arrived home all right, then again on Tuesday to say he wouldn't be able to come out to the farm, that he had a special meeting with his mechanics. She thought he might show up Wednesday night to help with the kids, but at seven o'clock, he still wasn't there.

Standing in the middle of the pasture, Dana watched Katie and Billy trot their horses in circles. She'd had to call Cindy and change her riding time to Thursday. With Windrunner laid up, she had only two horses to use, but plenty of time to give lessons—at least for a while. In two months the farm would belong to the bank. After that, she and her folks would be looking for a new home.

When she'd left the motel Monday, she'd still had hope that Windrunner's leg would be better, that it was a pulled muscle, not a tendon, and that a few days' rest was all it needed. Connie hadn't even placed at Sparta, her horse having knocked over a barrel, and there were still only twenty points separating their scores. The championship hadn't been won yet. But when Dana picked up her horse Monday afternoon, those hopes had died. His leg was worse, not better. Watching him limp into the trailer, she knew he wouldn't be running for a long time to come. Maybe never again. All because she'd wanted to win.

Tuesday she stayed home from work to take Windrunner to her own veterinarian. He'd kept the horse for X rays and observation. Tonight, over the telephone, he'd given her a ray of hope. The damage wasn't permanent; Windrunner wouldn't have to be put down. Weeks of rest, then a slow return to work and her horse would be as good as new. She could pick him up Friday.

Dana was relieved. She loved that horse. She'd asked so much of him over the past few months, and he'd always given, always tried. That she'd made it as close to winning the twenty thousand as she had was because of him.

She watched Katie try to urge HoJo into a canter and grinned. That old horse had also been a dear friend. He might not have the speed Windrunner had, but he had heart. "Kick with your outside leg," she yelled at Katie. "He's just feeling lazy tonight."

"Sit up straight, Billy." Danny's pony, Charlie, had a nice slow canter and if Billy would sit back, he'd be fine.

Ideally, she would like to have bought more horses, built an indoor ring and expanded her program. What she'd be doing was canceling it . . . and maybe finding new homes for her horses.

She'd told each of her riders' parents about the other riding schools for the handicapped. They'd said they would stay with her as long as she was there, that their children loved her. It was their support that kept her going.

After the horses were put out to pasture and the children had left, Dana aimlessly puttered around the barn. She felt lost. No longer was she gearing up for a weekend of rodeos. No longer was she busy training Windrunner. At last she had plenty of free time.

So, where was Garth?

It was nearly nine o'clock when she heard a car coming down the gravel road. Hanging up the bridle she'd finished cleaning, she listened to the vehicle's tires crunch over the small stones in its path. Her body was tense, waiting, and her heartbeat pulsed in her ears. It sounded like Garth's Bronco, but she might just be hoping.

Then the car stopped, and Dana hurried out of the barn.

Garth parked the Bronco next to her house, got out and started toward her door.

"Down here!" she yelled from the barn doors.

He looked her way, waved and headed in her direction. Silhouetted by the yard light, he strolled leisurely toward her, and Dana stood where she was, drinking in his manly proportions, an excited quiver in her stomach. For two nights she'd had trouble falling asleep. For two nights she'd lain alone in her bed, remembering a shower shared, a king-size bed and hours of lovemaking. For two nights she'd wanted to repeat the experience. Now Garth was here.

He held open his arms, and Dana moved forward to step into them. Their lips met and he gave her a long, satisfying kiss. "Howdy, pardner," he drawled when he finally lifted his head.

"Howdy, yourself." She laughed. "You're starting to sound like a cowboy."

"It's the company I keep." He slipped his arm around her shoulders. "Your folks up at the house?"

"As far as I know they are. Want to go to my place?" There they would have more privacy.

Her sultry invitation promised pleasure, but it would have to wait, at least for a while. He had a proposition to make. "Maybe later. Let's go talk to your folks. I think there's a way to save this farm."

"Save the farm? How?" She'd given up hope.

Garth started for the farmhouse on the hill, with Dana by his side. "I went to see your neighbour, Hal Hoffman, tonight. I remembered how upset he'd been about a junk car ordinance being enacted."

"A lot of the farmers are. They've kept the old cars and trucks for parts. Now they're being forced to get rid of them."

"Well, Hal took me around, and I met some of your other neighbors. They showed me what they have that the township's demanding they get rid of. I think maybe we can work out an arrangement where we can help them and they can help us."

"How?" she asked again.

IN HER PARENTS' HOME everyone, including Danny, was seated around the kitchen table, mugs of coffee and cans of Coke in front of them, while Garth explained how.

"Those old junkers are worth money: some simply as scrap metal, others if they were fixed up. I explained that to everyone I talked to tonight, but they said they didn't care, they weren't going to do anything with them, that having them around was going to cost them plenty and if it would help you keep this farm, they'd be glad to donate them to you. Seems you've got a lot of friends around here."

"They're good people," Dan Allen agreed. "Some are in the same trouble I am."

Dana could understand why the farms were willing to help. The cars and trucks the township supervisor wanted removed all had major problems; otherwise they wouldn't have been sitting around for years and wouldn't now be considered general eyesores. The few parts the farmers might be able to use from any of them wouldn't equal in value the stiff fines imposed by the new ordinance. The farmers had until the end of the year to get rid of the vehicles. Garth's offer to take them off their hands was probably just what they'd been hoping for.

"The question is, are you willing to turn your farm into a junkyard for a while and your equipment barn into an auto shop?" posed Garth.

"You think you can pick up enough to make it worthwhile?" asked Dana. The amount they needed to bring the total in their savings account to twenty thousand was just under thirteen thousand. As scrap metal, junkers were bringing around twenty-five dollars each. Considering the condition of most of the cars she'd seen sitting around, she couldn't imagine anyone paying much more than that.

Garth looked at her and nodded. "I think so. I didn't see any classics, but there were a few models that collectors like."

"What about that old truck of Hal's?" She knew Garth had been interested in it. Others might be also.

He grinned and shook his head. "He wasn't about to part with that baby. No, we'll just have to be content with what we can get. Those we can't get running, we'll strip down to the frame. Restoration specialists are always looking for parts, especially parts for scarcer models. And you'd be surprised what a market there is in accessories— even license plates. Early historical plates can bring as much as one hundred dollars."

"A hundred dollars—" Dana's mother gasped "—for an old license plate?"

Garth hurried to let her know that was only for rare ones.

"But isn't it going to cost a lot to get those cars from the farms to here, not to mention getting them running? And how are we going to get rid of them once they are here?

People aren't going to drive out to this farm for a used car. Dad will be the one who ends up with all the junkers." Dana hated playing the devil's advocate, but she saw a lot of flaws in Garth's plan.

"Your dad isn't going to end up with any junkers, at least not if I can help it," Garth assured her. "And, as far as the cost goes, I've talked to my mechanics. One is an old car buff, like myself, while a couple others are into racing. The four of us would be willing to put in extra hours after work and on weekends. The only thing they ask is for first dibs on any parts they might be able to use in their own projects. As for the cost of the tow trucks—" he shrugged and nonchalantly sipped his coffee "—I'll cover that."

Dana knew it wasn't the first time he'd donated the use of his tow truck for her. It was too much to ask. "We can't let you do that."

"Yes, you can." He smiled. "There are certain advantages to owning one's own garage. Let me enjoy them."

She played with her Coke. Garth had proven that when he wanted his way, he got it. There was no use arguing with him. But he hadn't solved their major problem. "How do we get rid of these cars and parts?"

"Hal said there's a special celebration in Clay at the end of October."

"Harvest Day," Dana's mother said, leaning forward to explain. "It's held the last Saturday in October every year. Starts with a parade and ends with a big dance—actually two dances, since the kids have one in the high-school gym and we old fogies get together for a square dance."

"And there are flea markets and craft booths?" Hoffman had told him there would be.

"Under tents put up in the village park. You think the people coming to Harvest Day will buy enough car parts and accessories to make thirteen thousand?" Dana's father sounded skeptical.

"Not so much those people coming to Harvest Day, though they'll buy some, but collectors and specialists. If we can get the word out that we've got cars and parts, they'll come."

ONCE THE IDEA was presented, it became a reality. Starting the next evening, Dan and Nancy Allen's family farm became a junkyard. During the day Dana's mother called neighbors, made the proposition and scheduled pickup dates and times. In the evening two of Garth's mechanics drove the tow trucks and made the pickups, then Garth and his men went over each vehicle while Dana cataloged it in. Some of the cars and trucks could only be classified as salvage metal and were dragged to one side to be hauled off and sold to a junkyard. Others had parts that could be used and were tagged to be dismantled. And a dozen— Chevies, Fords, Pontiacs and even one old Volkswagen Beetle—were deemed repairable and pulled into the equipment barn to be worked on. After a while the neighboring farmers were also helping, using their tractors to tow the cars the few miles to the farm, then sticking around to loosen bolts, clean parts and do whatever else was asked of them.

Garth brought out some of the equipment he'd already bought for his new garage and installed it in the barn. Dana found she was an accountant during the day and a mechanic at night. Her hours of working on the old Ford helped when she teamed up with Garth to take apart and put back together a 1961 Ford Falcon sedan. Carefully Garth removed each part of the engine, instructing her on where to put it so they'd know exactly where it went when they were ready to put the car back together.

"You know a car can contain as many as seventy thousand individual components," he said, pulling out one more. "If you're not careful, you can end up with a few in the wrong places. That's one reason a lot of collectors don't want to buy a car that needs much work. Unless they have the knowledge, a good working area and the proper equipment, it can be a time-consuming, frustrating and expensive job."

"But you love it, right?" She remembered the pictures he'd shown her of his Thunderbird. The car had been a mess when he bought it.

He grinned, handing her another part. "Right. For me, taking them apart and putting them back together is the challenge. I'd love to get ahold of that pickup Hal has. It's not in real bad shape, but it would need quite a bit of work and would be a dandy to own."

"But he wouldn't sell it to you?"

Garth gave a short laugh. "Honey, that man knows what that truck's worth. I didn't even make an offer."

Hour after hour, day after day, they worked on the Falcon, chatting and laughing. And in other sections of the barn, Garth's three mechanics, her father, Danny and an ever-changing number of neighbors also worked, tearing apart and putting engines back together, scraping away rust spots, filling them in, cleaning and mending seat covers and doing whatever else was necessary to get the cars— and the one truck—looking presentable again. And while they worked, Dana's mother brought them pots of coffee and fresh-baked pies—primarily apple during the month of September, then pumpkin in October.

By the end of October, most of Clay township's junk cars were gone. A semi had hauled away the scrap metal, with the proceeds paying the few bills they'd run up. Garth's mechanics took the parts they needed and two flatbeds were loaded with the remaining used-car parts, hubcaps, hood ornaments and old license plates. Collector clubs throughout Michigan, Indiana, Illinois and Ohio had been notified by letter of the Harvest Day sale. A list had been included of the most tempting items, along with a description of the cars that would be for sale and their condition. There were ten altogether, ranging from a 1957 Chevy Bel-Air that was in very poor condition to the Ford Falcon that Garth and Dana had worked on.

THE NIGHT BEFORE Harvest Day, long after the sun had set, Dana leaned against the pasture fence, watching Windrunner graze. Billowing clouds occasionally crossed the moon, their passage making it almost impossible for her to see the horse, and a cold breeze cut through her denim jacket. This was the weekend she should have been in Detroit, competing for the regional finals. Even though Connie Birch had continued doing poorly, she was going to win the money and the use of the truck. No one else was close enough in points to overtake her. Connie had called the week after the Sparta rodeo to ask how Windrunner was and if she'd be at the Charlotte Frontier Days rodeo, the final sanctioned rodeo whose points would count toward the championship. Dana was sure she heard the teenager sigh in relief when she said no, but she appreciated the call, anyway. Being competitors didn't mean they had to be at each other's throats.

Dana looked toward the equipment barn. Light shone through the cracks and she knew Garth was still in there giving everything a final check. Tomorrow was the big day. By evening they'd know if they'd made enough money to pay the bank or not. Her father had been confident they would. He'd planted his winter wheat and was already figuring out how much fertilizer he'd need for his crops and how many calves they'd be raising. She hoped he was right. If they failed, it wouldn't be for a lack of trying.

Her eyes moved on to the farmhouse. All the lights were out there except one in Danny's room. Her mom and dad had been tired and were probably already asleep, but Danny would be reading one of the farm journals he loved to pour over. The boy was meant to be a farmer; it was in his blood.

A noise brought her eyes back to the equipment barn. It was dusk now, but there was enough light for her to see Garth pull the doors closed, stuff his hands into the pockets of his aviator jacket and start for her house. "Down here!" she yelled, turning to lean against the fence and watch him change direction and head her way.

"How's he doing?" Garth asked as he neared, nodding toward the grazing horse.

"Better every day. The vet said it would be a good idea to give him another week or two of rest, then start longeing him. If the leg holds up, I should be able to get on his back by the end of November."

"Think you'll have him ready for that big rodeo in Tulsa?"

"The IFR?"

Garth nodded, stopping beside her. He'd learned that competing in the International Finals Rodeo was the goal of IPRA cowboys and cowgirls. Besides the money and prizes, there was the honor. Simply being there meant you were among the top in your profession.

"Let's take one day at a time," she suggested. After Windrunner's injury, she'd stopped even thinking about competing there. "Everything ready for tomorrow?"

"As ready as it's going to be, I guess." Garth rested his elbows on the top rail, and Dana turned back to her original position. In silence they both watched the lone horse graze. Finally Garth took in a deep breath, held it for a second, then let it out. "Dana, do you love me?"

Her eyes darted to his face. He wasn't looking at her, he was looking straight out. Chewing on her lower lip, she also let her eyes go back to probing the darkness. It took her several seconds before she answered. "Yes."

He did look at her then, but he didn't move his body. "Why haven't you ever said so?"

"Because . . ." She wasn't really sure how to explain. Looking his way, she shrugged. "I guess because you never said it to me—again."

He gave a short laugh. "The one time I did, I thought you were going to head for parts unknown."

"And, I guess," she continued, "because I was afraid to."

"Why would you be afraid to tell me you love me?" She had him confused.

She turned slightly to reach up and touch his chin with her fingertips. She could feel the stubble of his day's growth of beard. "Now that I've told you I love you, what? What happens next?"

"I ask you to marry me."

"That's what I was afraid of." Her hand dropped back to her side, and again she looked out across the field. "I still don't know if it will work between us."

"We've been getting along pretty well for the past two months, haven't we?" he challenged, sliding an arm around her shoulders.

"Sure, with you coming out here all the time, and me no longer rodeoing. And admit it, you don't like the same kind of music I like, and you're not wild about my singing."

Considering her singing, he did have to chuckle. "Let's put it this way, you have taught me to appreciate good music."

She grunted, understanding his meaning.

"As for the rodeoing, I'm not against your going to rodeos, I just didn't like the way you were pushing yourself, taking chances." Then he sighed. "No, you're right, I wouldn't want you going every weekend."

That was actually the least of her worries. She didn't want to be going every weekend, either. "It's our personalities, Garth. You're . . . citified. I'm countrified."

"And never the twain shall meet, eh?" In silence he stared out into the darkness, then finally he gave her shoulders a squeeze. "You know what else, we're both going to be *petrified* if we stand out in this cold much longer." Turning her toward him, he looked down at her face, then dipped his head and touched his lips to hers. "Like you said, honey, let's take it one day at a time. I'm ready for bed; how about you?"

"Sounds good to me." She stood on her toes and kissed him back, then slipped her arm through his.

"Have your folks ever said anything about the nights I've been spending here?" he asked, heading her up the hill toward her house.

"Nothing to me. I did hear Mom on the phone the other day, talking to my aunt. She didn't know I was in the kitchen, and she said it was the modern way and you were a nice person, so it didn't bother her."

"Good, because I have no intentions of driving back to town tonight, then out here in the morning."

Inside the warmth of her house, he pulled her to him, wrapping his arms around her slim waist. "I do love you, Dana Allen."

"And I love you," she murmured in response, tipping her head back to greet his lips.

She just wasn't sure that love was enough.

EARLY THE NEXT MORNING she fixed them breakfast, then hurried down to the barn to saddle HoJo and Charlie and load them into the trailer. Her students would be in the parade this year.

The temperature was cool, and clouds drifted across the blue sky. The weatherman, however, had promised a nice day. Dana hoped he was right.

One of Garth's mechanics came out—the car buff—and several local teenagers and neighbor farmers arrived to help Garth and her dad drive the nine recently restored cars and one truck into Clay. Her mother and Danny weren't driving but were going along as passengers. Dana prayed they'd all make it. In the barn the engines had sounded good, and the vehicles had all been given test drives up and down the gravel road, but this would be the first time any of them had gone any distance. As the first car moved out of the yard, she crossed her fingers.

Hal Hoffman drove the truck pulling the flatbeds loaded with parts, and Dana followed with her truck and trailer. As they pulled away from the farm, Windrunner trotted up and down the fence line, nickering to go along. It gave her a good feeling to look in her side-view mirror and see her horse moving without a trace of a limp.

On the way to Clay, she passed the 1938 Ford V-8 half-ton truck Garth had worked on just two nights before. It was already stalled by the side of the road. She stopped and picked up the driver—one of the boys who'd helped with the hay—and took him into town. There he went to find Garth. Dana had to leave the car problems up to him; she needed to make sure her riders were ready.

The restored cars and trucks were assigned positions in the parade just ahead of the horses, ponies and wagons. Walking between her two horses—Billy on Charlie and the two girls riding double on HoJo—Dana couldn't really tell what was going on ahead of her, but whenever the parade line slowed or came to a halt, she worried that it was because one of the cars had quit.

"Why have we stopped?" asked Billy, cocking his head to the side in an attempt to hear what was going on ahead.

"I wish we had candy to throw like those kids in the wagon. I'm gonna get down and get some candy," said Katie, and was almost off HoJo's back before Dana stopped her.

"You don't need any candy. Your mom will get you something to eat as soon as the parade's over. I don't know what's wrong, Billy. I can't see."

"Neither can I," he said and laughed, reaching forward to pat Charlie's neck.

By the end of the route they hadn't passed any stalled cars, and Dana felt relieved. Her three riders' parents claimed their hungry children, and Dana reloaded her horses and drove them back to the farm, unloaded them, unhitched the trailer and drove back into town. Then she proceeded to look up Garth.

The flatbeds with the car parts had been parked on the street in front of the village park, right in line with the big tent that had been erected for the craft booths and flea market. There were a lot of people looking over the parts they'd taken from the old junkers, mostly men but some women. Dana had promised to help that afternoon. Checking the cash box, she was surprised to see how much money they'd already collected.

"A supplier stopped by right after the parade," Garth told her. "We had a lot of things he was looking for. I'd hoped we would."

"How about the cars?" she asked. They'd been parked in the adjacent store's lot and her father was there, talking to anyone who showed an interest.

"We've sold two." He showed her the checks. "Got two thousand, one hundred for the Falcon. More than I'd expected. And two hundred fifty for the truck."

"Two hundred fifty?" Considering its condition, she was surprised they'd gotten even that much.

"Maybe I sold it too low, but the kid who drove it up here was the one who wanted it." He put the checks back into the box. "Call me a soft touch."

"Hmm, I don't know, sometimes you're pretty hard." She grinned at her own joke, then felt the color rising to her cheeks and quickly turned away and walked over to a man who was holding up four hubcaps.

By the time the day was over, they had sold six of the ten vehicles and most of what was on the flatbeds. Dana couldn't believe it. People had bought items she'd considered totally unsalable—pieces of chrome, bolts and door handles. After supper, sitting around the kitchen table in her parents' home, she tallied up the checks and cash for their deposit slip.

"Thirteen thousand, nine hundred thirty-one dollars and fifty cents," she finally announced, then sat back in her chair, staring at the figure she'd just read. They'd made it. With her winnings and the calf money, they actually had more than twenty thousand. The payments would be up-to-date, the bank wouldn't foreclose and the way things were going—at least if her father continued following her advice on financial matters—the farm was out of trouble.

"I think I can sell the other four cars," Garth said, leaning back in his chair. He'd put in a lot of hours and was tired. Dead tired. "I'll tow them into Kalamazoo and put them on the lot. I'll bet all of them are sold before the end of the year."

"I think any money you make off those cars should go to you," suggested Dana's mother, finally sitting down. "You and your men put in a lot of hours getting those cars and that old truck going."

"Your neighbors helped, too," he reminded her. "How would you feel if I gave each of my men a bonus, then took the remaining money and set up an account here in town that could be used by any farmer who found himself in a position like you were in?"

"You know, Dad," Dana added, looking up from the figures in front of her, "I was reading an article about a farm community that set up its own credit union. All the farmers in the area invested in it and went to it for loans. It might be something to consider here in Clay."

"Might be, indeed," he agreed. "I'll mention it tonight at the dance. You two comin'?"

At the idea of getting changed and going to a dance, Garth groaned.

Dana laughed and reached over to pat his hand. She didn't want to spend the evening in a crowded hall, listening to a caller and trying to remember steps she hadn't done for a year. What she wanted was some time with Garth, alone. "Tonight, Dad, I think we're just going to watch television and relax."

"So are all our problems solved now?" asked Danny, finishing a second piece of the pumpkin pie his mother had made.

"All but one," Garth answered, looking at Dana. "And I'm working on that one."

DANA HAD THOUGHT Garth would spend Sunday with her, that they'd finally be able to enjoy a day when neither of them had anything to do, but as soon as he'd had his morning coffee and breakfast, he told her he had to leave. With a hug and a kiss, he was gone. He didn't ask her to go with him or say when he'd be back, and she didn't ask. He'd spent so many hours out at the farm, she felt he deserved some time on his own. And she was sure he would be back. Yet, watching his tan Bronco disappear down the road, she experienced an empty feeling that bothered her.

By one o'clock the sky was entirely clouded over, and the threat of rain or snow was heavy in the air. Looking at the thermometer outside her kitchen window, Dana bet on snow, and by one-thirty it had started. Large, fluffy white flakes silently drifted down from the sky, melting as soon as they touched the ground.

She loved the first snow of the season. It didn't matter how many Michigan winters she went through or how much she'd cursed the ice and snow the February before, the first snow of the season always delighted her. Pulling on a heavy jacket, gloves and a scarf, she headed for the pond, walking at a fast enough clip to stay warm, but slow enough to be able occasionally to tilt her head back and catch a snowflake on the tip of her tongue.

The cold air was invigorating, clearing the cobwebs from her mind. As she neared the pond, the snow started coming harder, the flakes getting smaller and denser and beginning to stick. Fields of recently harvested corn were taking on a frosting of white. In the distance crows cawed, and when she reached the pond, she frightened into flight a gaggle of Canada geese, late in their travels south. Honking to each other, they flapped their large wings and rose into the sky, grouped, then formed a V and flew over the woods and out of sight. Dana watched them go, then stared into the water, its smooth surface reflecting her surroundings.

It hadn't been that long ago she'd pulled Garth into this pond. The water temperature had been cold that day; it would be downright freezing now, what with ice already forming near the banks. Garth had never gone back into the pond, and she doubted he ever would.

"Garth Roberts." She said the name aloud and a red squirrel in a nearby tree chattered back.

"Dana Roberts," she tried, and again the squirrel answered.

The name had a nice ring. *Mrs. Garth Roberts.* He'd asked her to marry him; she loved him and he loved her. Any woman in her right mind would say yes. So why hadn't she?

Because I'm afraid, Dana admitted to herself.

Pacing around the pond, hands behind her back, head down and her feet crunching on dry leaves, Dana silently rehashed all the pros and cons to marrying Garth. Then it came to her. She really had no choice. Life without Garth wouldn't be living at all. Her decision made, she headed back to her house.

She wanted to talk to Garth, but he wasn't at his apartment when she telephoned. Dana cursed when she heard the click, then, "Hi. Sorry..." Immediately she hung up.

This wasn't a message to be left on an answering machine.

Twenty minutes later, when Garth pulled up in front of her place, Dana realized why he hadn't been home to answer her call. He'd been on his way back to see her. Not even bothering to grab her coat or put on her boots, she ran out in her stocking feet, flung her arms around his neck and, lifting herself up on her toes, kissed him. "I love you and yes I want to marry you," she declared in one continuous stream of words, then kissed him again.

"Wow! Now that's the kind of greeting a man likes." He wrapped his arms around her and held her against his body, his eyes bright with pleasure as their lips kept touching. And then he felt her shiver with the cold and pushed her back slightly so he could look at her.

"You don't have any boots on . . . or a jacket." He shook his head. "And what brought about your sudden change of heart?"

"You." She again snuggled close to his warmth, this time putting her stocking-clad feet on his shoes so she was off the snow. However, his body didn't block all the cold air, and she couldn't stop shivering.

"Let's go inside before you turn into an icicle." He stepped toward the house, letting her ride on his shoes, his arms around her waist keeping her in place.

"Garth, I've thought it all over," she said, finally turning to lead the way into her house. "Since we met, you've made lots of sacrifices for me. It's time I started making a few. I'm willing to move into your apartment."

"Are you, now." He grinned and walked over to the hook that held her winter jacket. "Get your boots on, we're going for a ride."

"If you say so, boss." Saucily she sauntered over to where she'd left her boots. It was marvelous to have all her problems behind her. The farm was taken care of, Wind-runner was getting better, and best of all, she was in love, loved, and one day—hopefully soon—would be married.

"So now you're ready to move into my apartment. What happened while I was away to change your mind?" He held out her jacket and waited as she slid her feet into the boots.

"I went for a walk, that's all. Where are we going? To your place?"

"It's a surprise. And where'd you go for this walk?"

"Just to the pond and back. After you left, I guess I realized how lonely life would be without you." She put on her jacket as they left her house. "Funny, not all that long ago I really thought I was doing just great on my own. Then I met you."

"All because of a bad wheel-bearing." He opened the car door for her.

"All because of a bad wheel-bearing," Dana repeated, remembering that night. She was smiling when he got in on the driver's side. "And all because you agreed to help a damsel in distress."

He chuckled. "I almost didn't."

"Any regrets?" Her eyes mirrored her concern.

Garth shook his head, then leaned over to kiss her before starting the Bronco's engine. "Falling in love with a cowgirl has definitely been an interesting experience." Turning on the windshield wipers, he cleared away a thin layer of freshly fallen snow, then backed out of her yard. "I'm still wondering what changed your mind about moving into my apartment."

"Well, I won't say I'm wild about the idea, but I don't see any other alternative—at least not right now. So, if you still love me—" and she hoped he did "—then I'll move in with you."

"I still love you," he assured her, reaching across the seat to take her hand and give it a squeeze. "And I still want to marry you."

"Anytime." When they'd met, she'd told him she wouldn't have time for a man until November. Well, it was now November. "From now on we do what you want."

"I think . . ." He paused because he knew what he was about to suggest would mean he wouldn't be seeing much of her until after January. He'd have to be second in her life again. Still, it was the only thing to do. "I think," he began anew, "if Windrunner is all right, what I want is for you to get him back into training and win that world championship."

"Garth, do you realize what you're saying?"

"How many times are you going to have this chance?" he asked.

She doubted it would come again. She didn't want to go through another year of pushing herself as she had this season. Some people relished that kind of pressure; she didn't.

As Garth drove north from her place, back toward Battle Creek, they talked about the possibility of her competing in the International Finals Rodeo. She tried to make him understand the time it would take to get the horse back in shape. He merely listened and nodded. And when they were almost to the freeway that connected Kalamazoo and Battle Creek, he turned onto a gravel road. Then, less than a hundred yards down, Garth turned the wheel again, heading up a dirt drive toward a small white house. A For Sale sign was stuck in the lawn in front of the house, a blob of snow covering the S and making it For ale. A single-car garage and a large red barn were set back and slightly to the side. Garth stopped in front of the house.

"What do you think?" he asked, turning off the car's motor.

"I think I wouldn't have a chance for the championship."

"So, you go for the fun of it. Now, what do you think of this place?"

Dana looked around the yard. The falling snow actually helped dress up the run-down house and outbuildings, yet it had an appeal—like that of an abandoned puppy one couldn't turn away from. The garage and barn looked in the best shape, though even they had a few holes here and there where boards had been broken or had rotted out. "Does someone live here?" It seemed doubtful.

"No, it's vacant. Twenty acres come with the place, most of them either tillable or good for pasture. At least that's what the realtor said. And there's a small creek that cuts across the land." *But no pond,* he thought, thankful for that. "It's only three miles from a ramp to the freeway, ten minutes to work for me, ten minutes for you."

Realizing what he was suggesting, Dana looked around again. Yes, the place did have an appeal. And she couldn't have asked for a better location. It might need a lot of work, but they could do it. They'd already proven they could work well as a team.

"Want to look at the inside?"

"Sure," she said eagerly. Then, tempering her enthusiasm, she put a hand on his sleeve, stopping him from getting out of the car. "How can we afford it, Garth?"

"Let's look around first, then we can talk finances." He slipped his hand into his jacket pocket and pulled out a key. "The realtor said to take our time."

Inside the little house, Dana walked through each room checking out closets and cupboards, while Garth jumped on floors and thumped walls to test for sturdiness. Cobwebs caught in her hair, all the walls needed to be stripped, painted or papered, and some of the windows and doors would have to be replaced, but the basic structure was sound. When they were finished, they stood in the middle of the living room, in front of the stone fireplace. "Well?" asked Garth.

"It's going to take a lot of work," she admitted.

"Think we could do it? Or, rather, are you game to?"

She grinned, realizing that this house, no matter how poor its shape, was exactly what she wanted. "Definitely. A little soap and water, some paint and elbow grease, and this will be a dream house."

"Good." He'd hoped she'd like it. He certainly did. "As soon as I sell the T-Bird, we can sign the papers."

Dana felt her hopes sink. "Garth, no. You can't sell your car."

"Honey, it's the only way I can make the down payment."

He didn't want her regretting not having gone to the finals. Well, she didn't want him sacrificing his car. Shaking her head, she repeated "No."

He walked over and put his hands on her hips. "Dana, I won't be selling it just because of the house. You know I want that 1938 Baby Mack Hal Hoffman has in his garage. Well, yesterday he said he'd sell it to me. I've enjoyed owning the T-Bird, but now I'm ready for something new."

"You're sure?" she pursued.

"I'm sure." He kissed her and held her close. "Dana, I think I'd like living out here. It's as close to a compromise as I've been able to find. We're not in the city, but it's not that far away. And you could bring Windrunner here and work him, and I'd see you every night." He kissed her again. "Every night."

THE STEADILY FALLING SNOW outside hadn't kept the crowds away. The announcer had already said this was the largest turnout ever for an International Finals Rodeo. Garth could believe it. The stands were filled to capacity. Leaning against the railing, he watched a red pickup enter the arena, three fifty-five-gallon barrels and two men on the bed. Another few minutes and those barrels would be in place and the first of five cowgirls would come through the alleyway. They'd be making their fifth and final go-round. He hated to admit it, but he was nervous.

"She's gonna make it," said Sharon, coming up beside Garth.

Cody was right behind her, five-month-old Tammye cradled on his hip. "The way I see it," he said, "the least she can get is second."

"She won't be second," promised Garth, crossing his fingers as Dana always did.

"Now, that's the confidence we like to see." Sharon took his arm and gave it a squeeze, then slipped back beside her husband, reaching over to brush a lock of blond hair back behind her daughter's ear.

"Congratulations to you," Garth offered to Cody. "Those were tough broncs you rode."

The cowboy smiled. "Not as tough as those steers, I guess. I can't believe I missed that one Friday night."

The baby reached for the brim of Cody's cowboy hat, and Garth chuckled at the little girl's intense expression. She'd changed a lot from the wrinkled, red-faced infant he'd met in a Grand Rapids hospital. Her complexion was now a smooth peaches and cream; her body had filled out and grown; short, thick blond hair covered most of her head and she smiled constantly. Just looking at the baby made him long for one of his own; only his would have dark hair, with reddish highlights, just like Dana's. And probably her dark eyes. In a way he hoped so. He never tired of looking into Dana's eyes.

"Nervous?" asked Sharon.

"Who, me?" Garth looked back at the arena. They had two of the barrels in place. One more to go. "Heck, I'm getting to be an old pro at this."

Sharon let her gaze skim over him, from his rumpled hair to the toes of his leather boots. They were dress boots, not cowboy boots. "I see Dana still hasn't turned you into a cowboy."

"And I don't think she ever will." Not that they argued about it anymore. Dana had accepted their differences. "I'm the mechanic and she's the cowgirl. I keep the truck running so it can get us here, and she wins the money so we can buy a new one."

"And maybe she'll win a little extra so you two can get married?" Sharon cocked her head, grinning knowingly.

"We're doing that whether she wins or not. You'll be getting an invitation."

"She already told me," Sharon confessed.

"Ladies and gentlemen, the event we've all been waiting for, one of the most popular events at any rodeo . . . cowgirls' barrel racing."

Applause greeted the announcer's call.

"And before today is over, we're going to have a new world champion. From the northeastern region, Dana Allen, whose horse, Windrunner, suffered a serious injury last September and has made a miraculous comeback. And from the western region . . ."

Garth felt a knot form in his stomach. This afternoon he wasn't sure if the tension he felt was for her safety or because he wanted so badly for her to win. Absently he ran his fingers through his hair, his eyes directed toward the alleyway that Dana and Windrunner would come through. He'd wanted to stay with her, but she'd insisted he come out and watch.

He'd never be relaxed about her competing—there was always that chance she could be hurt—but knowing how much she loved it, he'd endure the tension and support her. Still, he was glad she'd decided to make this her last year for serious competition. He'd never have forced her to give it up, but when she asked what he thought about buying some more horses and fixing up a ring so she could teach riding to handicapped children on the weekends, he'd readily agreed.

There were only five cowgirls left in the final go-round, but each had a chance to win the world title. The first cowgirl entered the arena through the alleyway, her horse running full out. One tight turn after another and she was on her way back. "Fifteen point nine two," the announcer called out.

Not a bad time, noted Garth. With these horses and riders, none of the times was likely to be bad. But he knew Dana could do better.

The next rider entered the arena, ran the pattern and ran out, using her bat to get the most speed out of her horse. "Fifteen point seven three," was the call.

"She could win the round, but she couldn't beat Dana's average," Sharon said, marking her program.

"The California gal's next," noted Garth. He knew she was the one who could beat Dana.

His fingers turned white as he gripped the railing and watched the willowy blonde from California push her horse from barrel to barrel. Whooping and hollering, she spurred the roan into a full gallop back to the time line.

"Fifteen point three nine."

"Each one's going faster," noted Cody, looking over his wife's shoulder as Sharon marked the time.

"Let's hope Dana keeps up the pattern."

He waited for Dana to enter the arena. His lungs hurt and his throat was so tight he could barely swallow. Ulcers were made from days like this. Owning and managing a growing auto-repair business involved no tension compared to standing helplessly on the sidelines and watching the one he loved race around those barrels. He could hardly breathe.

Dana held Windrunner back for a second, collecting herself. This was it. This was her one and only chance to go down in history as a world-champion barrel racer. She chewed on her lower lip and tried to calm the butterflies in her stomach. Windrunner danced, ready to go. She took a deep breath, then loosened the reins.

Like an arrow in flight, the chestnut gelding flew for the first barrel. The crowd in the stands was a blur. Dana grabbed the saddle horn and swung to the right and her horse pivoted within a hairbreadth of the can. "Go, go, go," she chanted, feeling Windrunner pour on the speed. A swing to the left and they were around the second barrel. "Yes, yes, yes," she sang to him as he stretched for the third. "We can do it, we can do it."

His hindquarters twisted around the third barrel, and for a brief second Dana feared she might be going too fast, that her horse might slip. Then he gathered himself and headed for the time line. Leaning forward she called his name. No crop was used, only words. Today they were a team—a world-champion team—a flying combination of red and blue.

And then they were out of the arena, their moment of glory over. The audience stood, yelled, applauded and shouted.

"Fourteen point three two," screamed the announcer. "Ladies and gentlemen, she just beat the best time by one full second."

"I told you she wouldn't be second," said Garth, and went to meet her halfway.

Harlequin Temptation

COMING NEXT MONTH

#209 WILDE 'N' WONDERFUL JoAnn Ross

During a summer on the road Sara McBride let Darius Wilde research her life-style—but she didn't have to like it! He had obviously set his sights on her as a lifetime travel companion, and *that* wasn't part of the deal....

#210 KEEPSAKES Madeline Harper

For Nora Chase, the customer was always right—that was what kept her personalized shopping service thriving. And David Sommer was one sexy customer who had his heart set on the ultimate gift: Nora.

#211 FOXY LADY Marion Smith Collins

Could a flamboyant nightclub singer with a teenage son relate to a conservative anthropology professor with a teenage daughter? Dani and Hamp soon discovered that the answer was a resounding and passionate "yes!"

#212 CAUSE FOR CELEBRATION Gina Wilkins

Overwhelmed by work, theme-party coordinator Merry James breathed a sigh of relief at the appearance of her supposed temporary secretary, Grant Bryant. But soon she suspected that his steamy glances meant he had more on his mind that typing and filing....

Temptation™

TEMPTATION WILL BE
EVEN HARDER TO RESIST...

In September, Temptation is presenting a sophisticated new face to the world. A fresh look that truly brings Harlequin's most intimate romances into focus.

What's more, all-time favorite authors Barbara Delinsky, Rita Clay Estrada, Jayne Ann Krentz and Vicki Lewis Thompson will join forces to help us celebrate. The result? A very special quartet of Temptations...

- **Four striking covers**
- **Four stellar authors**
- **Four sensual love stories**
- **Four variations on one spellbinding theme**

All in one great month! Give in to Temptation in September.

TDESIGN-1